Blind Water Pass

Anna Metcalfe

JM ORIGINALS

First published in Great Britain in 2016 by JM Originals
An imprint of John Murray (Publishers)
An Hachette UK Company

1

© Anna Metcalfe 2016

The right of Anna Metcalfe to be identified as the Author of the Work
has been asserted by her in accordance with the Copyright, Designs and
Patents Act 1988.

A CIP catalogue record for this title is available from the British Library

Trade Paperback ISBN 978-1-47363-181-6
Ebook ISBN 978-1-47363-182-3

Typeset in Sabon MT by Palimpsest Book Production Limited,
Falkirk, Stirlingshire

Printed and bound by CPI Group (UK) Ltd, Croydon, CR0 4YY

John Murray policy is to use papers that are natural, renewable and
recyclable products and made from wood grown in sustainable forests.
The logging and manufacturing processes are expected to conform to the
environmental regulations of the country of origin.

John Murray (Publishers)
Carmelite House
50 Victoria Embankment
London EC4Y 0DZ

www.johnmurray.co.uk

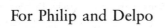

For Philip and Delpo

Contents

Blind Water Pass

Old Ghost

Sitting under the most pathetic of all the pathetic-looking foothill trees, by the mountains that marked the edge of the village, Old Ghost was teaching me how to play 'Crazy Eights'.

'You have too much imagination; not enough strategy,' he said. 'And you're going to lose.

❧

'We're out of wine,' says Rina, without looking in the fridge, so I know she has been drinking alone. Before I make any comment about it, she says: 'I'll go.' She throws on her coat and she goes.

❧

Old Ghost

Rina and I have three things in common: we are immigrants, we share a flat and we work irregular hours. Rina is an auxiliary nurse. I am a driver for the Hotel de L'Amitié, a plush hotel in the heart of the 5th arrondissement. We do not live in the city itself but in Ivry-sur-Seine, which has a good end and a bad end and two metro stops. Our basement flat is smack in the centre of it all and is neither good nor bad. It is very small. There are two small bedrooms, a shower closet, and a bit in the middle with a sofa, an old television and a coffee table; then a corner that we call the kitchen, complete with microwave, fridge and sink. We keep our food in a small cabinet under the television or on the floor.

Rina hates her job, handing out cups of water, taking urine samples and, in her words, cleaning up after everybody else. I like my job and I am respected for being reliable and available to work at all hours. Unlike the majority of my colleagues, I am not married and I do not have children. This is enough, for the moment, to make me a good employee. Mostly, I do transfers, delivering tourists to the gaudy hotel foyer or taking them back to the concrete bays

4

of the airport and the clunkiness of all things international. Other tasks include chauffeuring guests to
and from the major sites of interest: art galleries,
restaurants, *les grands magasins*.

❧

I like the monotony of my work, the familiar roadways, the predictability of my clients. There are
those who are silent, those who ask questions,
and those who wish to be asked the particular questions
that a taxi driver is allowed to ask: Is this your first
time in the city? Are you here on business? Will you
be staying long? I have cultivated an unshakeable
patience in the face of traffic jams, diversions and
roadworks. I talk just enough to be charming for
the sake of a decent tip but not so much that they
remember who I am when they get out of the car.
It is a strange kind of art.

❧

Rina comes back with the wine and pours it into
tumblers. She asks about my day and I tell her about
a client I had to take to the Botanical Gardens. When
we got there, he asked me to wait for him until he was
ready to return to the Hotel de L'Amitié. I didn't have
to wait very long. After ten minutes he reappeared,

moving towards the car almost at a run. His face was red and blotchy. As he got closer, I thought I saw a tear on one cheek but it might have been a drop of sweat gleaming in the afternoon sun. He appeared quite flustered, and before he got in the back, he stopped to slap himself on the face a couple of times. He was tall, fairly handsome and well dressed: an appearance that seemed suddenly incongruous given his emotional disarray. When he finally opened the door of the car, he could not wait to confess his embar-rassment. He explained, in English, how in the garden there was a series of large, banked flower beds with rows and rows of small yellow blooms growing close to the ground. They were the very same flowers that his mother had grown in the garden of his childhood home. As a boy, she had requested that, in the summer months, he urinate on the flowers to make them grow a little taller. A neighbour had told her the trick. He did as he was asked and, over time, the flowers did indeed increase in size and health. When he saw the very same flowers in the Botanical Gardens he felt an extraordinary urge to urinate over the whole damn lot, in honour of his mother. Torn between this desire – which, he wished to emphasise, was extreme – and the knowledge that this would be entirely inappropriate behaviour that could result in his being arrested or, at the very least, forced to leave, he fled the scene. It was the struggle between these two demands on his being at the gardens that was the cause of his distress.

On the way back to the hotel he pulled a set of clippers out of the inside pocket of his jacket and began to trim his finger nails. When we arrived at the hotel car park, he picked the small pieces of trimmed nail off his trousers and the seat of the car. He then placed them in a small, black pouch, which he returned to his inside pocket, along with the clippers. Later, when I inspected the car, it was almost spotless: just one tiny clipping of nail that I swept away with a tissue.

Rina says she does not know how I put up with all these imbeciles who have so much more money than sense. I say it makes things more interesting. Rina laughs.

'How was your day?' I say, but she ignores my question and talks again about her ex-husbands.

The first one is dead. Her biggest regret is that their marriage was almost over before he passed. She often says how, if only he'd died six months earlier, when things were all right, there'd be something to cling to. The second ex-husband, who is, in fact, technically still her husband, works with Rina at the hospital. He is a doctor. He is the reason she is here. They arrived together as economic migrants eighteen months into their marriage, just as the cracks in their relationship were beginning to show. They thought that if they could solve their money problems they could solve themselves. They were wrong. He left Rina for a twenty-year-old cook working in the hospital cafeteria, which means that Rina has to take a packed lunch with her every day. Now he has no money problems at all while Rina has far more than she ever had at home. But she won't go back. Too stubborn.

I never tire of telling her she will meet someone new, but Rina doesn't believe in these possibilities any more. After she has revealed her latest thoughts, she says it doesn't matter, it will all end up the same. Then she raises her hand and points a finger at me.

'Tell me about Old Ghost,' she says.

So I tell her the story of Old Ghost, which she has heard many times.

Tomorrow, I have to take a client to a place I have never driven to before, a fair way out of the city on the other side of Château de Vincennes. After

I have told Rina the story of Old Ghost, I take down the map to check the route, spreading it over the coffee table. There is a bend in the river that reminds me of the river back home, the lazy curve it draws through the city.

'Rina,' I say, 'is there anything here that makes you feel like you're somewhere else?'

'What do you mean?' she says.

'Like a building, a window, a view. Something that reminds you of a different place and trips you up.'

'The embassy,' she says.

'Which one?' I ask.

'Russian,' she says. 'The big, Soviet front. Looks like my old town hall. We had assemblies there some-times, for school, on special occasions.'

I feel glad that she has a connection to home and that the answer to my question came so readily. Certain places have a way of making other places more imaginable. Other places give the impression that their place is the only place on earth. Paris can do both, depending on the arrondissement, and the direction in which you are facing.

&

I don't trust maps anymore, though they have been the key to my survival in the city. If I picture a map of my homeland, I see the lines of its borders trembling, like the unfinished drawing of a child. Its mountainous regions and vast waterways are depicted in colours from smoke-grey to ink-black, and the whole surface of it pulses like an open wound. People trickle out of the borders leaving trails of inky black behind them, marking out pathways over adjoining territories. Spots of ink reach all corners of the globe: microscopic, black dots, like bugs behind the glass of a picture frame.

Among all the black dots, there is one dot in particular that troubles me. That is the one that marks the imagined movements of Old Ghost. The more I try to fix it, the more it shakes and wobbles until the whole thing becomes a terrible blur.

Old Ghost has taken on a particular significance for Rina, not as a person, but as an idea. It is not that he is alive or that he loves me that matters to her. It is the fact that she believes me when I say he is, or was, kind, and that his genre of kindness ever existed at all.

Old Ghost, I say to Rina, is the best man I have ever known. This is true, but I have not known very many men – at least, not very well. There is my brother, with whom I travelled and who also lives here, working in a bakery in the north part of the city. There is my father, now living on the other side of the world, with my mother, where they are safe. We no longer speak, as for a long time he feared that any communication could put us all in danger. Now, our silence has become habit. If I were to write to him, I would not know what to say. He is a spiritual man and believes that – with or without regular conversation or letter writing – somehow we are still in touch. My brother hates him for abandoning us, for assuming that we could make it on our own. He finds his spiritual optimism patronising and unrealistic, while I sit somewhere in the middle, wanting to believe in everything my father says, while understanding the impracticability and danger of his ideals.

These are the men I have known. And Old Ghost. Although I have not heard from him since the blackout, my guess is that he is still very kind.

'Tell me how you met,' Rina says.

'At the school gates,' I say. 'He was my brother's friend.'

❧

Actually, he was not my brother's friend; he was trying to become my brother's friend, but my brother was smart, popular and good at sport, which meant that he was also influential and could afford to be picky. Old Ghost, quiet and overly polite, did not fit in. For several weeks, Old Ghost persisted, waiting for my brother to leave school to see if he could go with him to the cinema or the ice-cream shop or the basketball courts, but my brother, despite under-standing his silent pleas, walked past every day without giving Old Ghost so much as a look.

I knew that it was best for me to walk behind, so that my brother could do as our parents bade him and drop me off at home, while at the same time pretending to have nothing to do with me. Old Ghost lived near us and, for a time, as I walked behind my brother, he walked a few paces behind me, placing himself beneath even me in the social rankings. Then one day he said hello and after that we walked together. This displeased my brother and made him suspicious, but it did not displease him sufficiently to talk to our parents – who were, after all, engaged in far more important affairs – or to take his mind off his own concerns regarding the maintenance of his high status at school, the same status that would, eventually, give him the contacts he needed in order for us to make our escape.

Whatever I can say about my brother, he was the

one to make sure I could get out while my father took care of my mother and himself, as ever, thinking it for the best to let us make it on our own.

'But when did you really make friends?' Rina wants the long version this time, with details and supporting evidence.

'There was a shop across the road from the school,' I say. 'I went in to buy a box of tea. Old Ghost followed me. He bought me a pack of cards. His father played a lot of cards and so he taught me his favourite games.'

'And you became friends,' Rina says.

'And we became friends. He was like a teacher to me.'

'A teacher or a friend?'

'He helped me with my homework. He made me creative. He was as patient a person as you can imagine. He listened to me. He helped me to picture my dreams and make them real and solid things that I could have and hold and do and achieve and be.'

'When did he give you the maps?' Rina says.

'You're skipping ahead,' I say.

Rina shrugs. She fills her empty glass and tops mine to the brim. Rina drinks fast.

'I was fifteen. We were starting to talk about how and when to leave.'

'When you say *we*.'
'My brother and I.'
'Not Old Ghost,' Rina says.
'No,' I say.
'Did you always know you would leave him?'
'No,' I say. I don't like this. She knows.
'So tell me about the maps.'
I tell her about the maps.

You couldn't get maps of foreign places – at least, not big ones with all the detail – unless they were specially ordered to the library. While my brother talked only about the practicalities of leaving, and never the reality of arriving somewhere else, I wanted some security. I knew there were many things for which I would not be able to prepare myself, but there were also things I could learn that would make life easier upon arrival. I could learn to find my way around the city, I decided, if only I had a map. So Old Ghost wrote a history project on this very place in order to get for me the maps that I required. I drew plan after plan of the roadways, some of which he used as illustrations in his work.

'And Old Ghost memorised the maps as well,' Rina says.

'No,' I say.

'So you always knew that he would not be coming?'

'No,' I say.

'But he didn't learn the roads? It doesn't make sense.'

'None of it makes sense. The whole thing is ridiculous. Would it ever occur to you to memorise a city you'd never seen?'

'No,' she says. 'How did you do it?'

I studied and I studied and I studied. It was a time in my life when I believed there was nothing I couldn't achieve by learning. Old Ghost held the maps up to his face and tested me. He would say things like: 'Take me from Canal Sainte-Thérèse down to Le Musée de l'Art Brut, and I would get annoyed because he was giving me too many clues.'

'What clues?' he would say.

And I would tell him: 'You said "down",' and he would apologise.

I would describe to him the roads and the roundabouts, the one-way systems and the lanes it was necessary to traverse in order to get from the one place to the other. Mostly, I was right. I had worked hard, after all. But if I made an error, he would always correct me, and always with kindness. He once said: 'Taxi drivers are usually men, you know,' but not in a way that made me think I couldn't do it. When he was old enough to use his father's car, he took me out to the disused corn fields and taught me how to drive an automatic. He said I was a quick learner, that there was nothing I couldn't do.

❧

'Why did he not leave when you left?' says Rina.

I know what she is doing: she is pushing me to feel something so that she can feel something too.

'I was in danger and he was not,' I say. 'My parents were in trouble with the government, and his were not.'

'But your parents thought you would be safe.'

'They thought that once they were gone we would be left alone. I would have believed them but my brother knew better.'

'And now?' Rina says. 'Will Old Ghost be safe now?'

I say nothing.

'Will he come, do you think? He knows where you are, after all.'

The question frightens me. Rina senses my fear and is herself afraid.

'He'll come,' she says, with a smile. 'I know it.'

'It's not that kind of story,' I say. 'He was like a brother.'

16

'You have a brother,' Rina says.
'A teacher, then.'
'You're too old for teachers, now.'
But these are the only kinds of men I can imagine.

I have changed my mind. I no longer wish to tell stories about the past. I want to talk only of the present; about my passengers and how, for a short time, I control the direction of their lives. They sit in the back of my car on the phone to this person, or that, or the other. They say things like: 'I'm here safely, I'll call again soon, I'll see you next week.' They complain about how expensive it is now to call abroad. It should all be the same price. What's a bit of land, a stretch of water?

'Show me a photograph,' says Rina, though she knows that I have none.
  I remember precisely when the photographs went missing. It was the first border crossing. The guards got us to unpack everything and then watched us as we packed it all up again. I had a small rucksack and, while pulling it onto my back, out of the corner of my eye I saw something fall. I think I knew the

photographs were gone. I could have bent down to look, to check it was not the photographs that were lying there on the ground, that it was just some tissues or an old receipt, but I did not. Rather, I climbed back into the truck with my brother, linking my arm through his. He does not like me to touch him but over the month-long journey he never once complained. In any case, we left, and when I look back now I wonder why I let the photographs go. I know that I must have done it on purpose, but I can't say why.

☙

As we travelled, things were changing in a way that I have only just begun to be able to describe. When travelling, it is difficult to note a shift in anything other than safety and terrain. With greater stability, however, it is possible to look back and mark the subtle changes that took place, remembering who I was before I left and taking stock of who I have become. I see now what I lost on the journey: some bright, essential thing, which gave me a kind of confidence I have not yet recovered.

I have decided that there are two different kinds of wanting to live. One is illogical, irrational and rude. It kicks in when there is nothing else left.

The other is beautiful: a desire to be, and a desire for others to be.

There are no maps for this terrain.

❧

Rina pours the last of the wine into her glass and retrieves the second bottle from the fridge.

'Do you still have the cards?' she says.

'The playing cards?' I say. This is a question she has not asked before.

'Yes,' she says.

I go to my room and pull the battered box of cards from the drawer in my bedside table.

'When did you last play?' Rina says.

'On the journey here. We played a lot. There wasn't much else to do.'

'Which games?'

'All kinds.'

'The ones Old Ghost taught you?' says Rina.

'Sometimes,' I say.

'Can you teach me one?' says Rina.

'Yes,' I say, shuffling the cards in my hands.

I place eight well-worn cards face down on the map-covered table and explain the rules.

Thread

'They're here,' said Saba.

'Yes,' he replied.

She opened the door. Three men were standing beside a truck in the yard. They nodded. She nodded back, then turned to her husband to say goodbye.

She did not allow herself to cry. Instead, she felt herself getting smaller, or the house getting bigger: the white-washed walls shooting up into the sky, the earthen floor levelling out like spilt coffee. Mussa took her in his arms and she shrank further.

He loaded two canvas bags onto the truck and clambered in after them. She couldn't see how many others were inside, only the shudder of grey tarpaulin as the truck pulled away, rolling down the city's northern slopes towards the border and then the desert.

It was five thirty, the sun was almost up. Saba waited in the yard. When the sound of the truck had faded into the hum of morning traffic, she closed the door, catching her dress in the frame. As she stepped back into the house, the fabric ripped. For a moment, Saba thought the tears would come cascading down her face, but she breathed heavily and kept them at bay. *Not yet,* she thought.

She stooped and pulled gently until the material of the dress came free. It was a white thing of delicate linen and the tear was in the seam, four inches long. Pale threads hung across it like a cobweb.

The house had two large rooms. There was the kitchen with its large wooden table, a sink and several low cupboards; then a small bedroom where they slept and kept their books – large volumes of poetry and prose from which they read to one another on Mussa's days off. He had made all the furniture – their bed, the kitchen table, the cupboards, the desk. Each piece was engraved with a line from one of her favourite poems.

Saba kept her sewing things in a box beneath the bed. She slid it out from between an old suitcase and Mussa's army boots. Her hands shook as she brought it to the table, spools of thread rattling against the thin case. Saba sat down and hitched up her skirt, smoothing the broken seam across the wooden surface. With hands splayed over the fabric, she steadied herself, leaning into the table. She opened the box and picked a needle from the pin cushion. Digging among the coloured reels, she pulled white thread from a spool and, in one swift motion, fed it through the needle's eye. Her hand drew wide circles as she sewed while her eyes kept flicking back to the door, half hoping that he might return, as he had before, after some problem. When she finished sewing, she knotted the thread and held up the fabric to look at her work. The join was clumsy, the stitches misaligned, but it would do. With the seam pulled taut between her hands she sat for a moment and did nothing.

She had hardly slept. In the night, she had touched Mussa's arm from time to time, whether to comfort him or herself she could not be sure. He remained completely still though she knew he was not asleep. Stillness was a choice that he made, his way of being calm.

Thread

They had been married a year. The first six months he spent in military service, working at the southern border, rebuilding the rail tracks that were damaged during the war. When he returned, his skin was darker, his hands rough and the whites of his eyes slightly clouded. He went back to his job at the furniture shop, building bespoke pieces for the city's richest families, but the work seemed to tire him in a way that Saba had not seen before. When the education reforms were imposed, teachers and students protested. Mussa had been in the centre of town that day, delivering an elaborate toy chest to an old barrister who had commissioned the piece as a gift for his granddaughter. As he was leaving, he had found himself caught up in the seething mob.

Mussa was not the only innocent bystander to be arrested; almost everyone knew someone. They held him for two months. He told her, repeatedly, not to visit him, as it was too dangerous, but he wrote to her every day. Whenever she felt on the verge of doing something rash, another letter would arrive, reassuring her that it would all be over soon. He returned paler and thinner, the muscles in his shoulders wasted and his eyes narrow.

He saw no future in the city, he said. He could no longer look forward. The essence of the place had altered and he was losing a sense of himself. Saba knew he had to find a way to leave, to get a job in another city, where one day she could join him.

In this period of rapid change, Saba had seen him scared, yes, but never fraught. He had been despondent but never inconsolable. He did things slowly and with purpose, as though protesting the city's atmosphere of uncertainty and deceit. His steadiness gave him an air of permanence. She pictured him, teeth clenched, back straight, as the truck skimmed the uneven track that led to the desert, a landscape Saba had never seen. She tried to conjure a version of it in her mind but could not. It existed beyond the places of safety to which her imagination clung: the two-room house, the kitchen table, the contents of the sewing box, the small round hollows inside the plastic reels of thread.

Several times, while Mussa was in prison, men from the military had come to search the house. They did not appear to be looking for anything in particular. They took money, demanded food, emptied drawers, cupboards and boxes. They drank the bottle of wine she had kept, left over from their wedding day. Saba was grateful that they ignored the books and everything else she considered of value.

The important things she kept in a shallow metal

tin under the sink, beneath a thick pile of newspapers. She fetched the tin and placed it on the table
by the sewing box, leaving the papers scattered across
the floor. Now there were two boxes open in front
of her: one was bright with threads and buttons,
with bits of ribbon spilling over the sides; the other
was filled with scraps of paper, old letters and an
occasional photograph.

The first poem that came to hand was the one she
had performed on her father's birthday. It was six
lines long – an Italian sestet – and scribbled on an
old receipt. Others had been written on loose sheets
of notepaper or blank pages she had torn from the
backs of books. Most of them remained familiar.
She read a few lines, raised her eyes from the page
and found the words were still flowing. These things,
she thought, would never leave her mind. Having no
further use for the paper on which the lines were
written, she placed them in a pile at one end of the
table.

A family photograph lay at the bottom of the tin
– both sets of grandparents, her mother and father,
sisters, aunts, uncles and cousins – taken when she
was seven years old, gap-toothed and laughing.
Balancing it on the tips of her fingers, she shivered
as she looked at the faces of people she loved, many

of whom had died in the conflict or, like Mussa, simply chosen to leave, having lost faith in the idea of a future in their own land.

She got to her feet, scooped a fistful of coffee beans from a jar on a high shelf and took them outside into the yard. She scattered the beans into a dark iron pan, stoked the fire and placed them over the heat. They hissed and emitted a heady steam, the aroma tickling her nose. She fetched the unwanted poems from inside and fed them, one by one, into the flames. While coffee brewed in the clay jebena, the scraps of paper curled to ashes, their edges glowing until they finally disappeared.

With the jebena in hand, Saba went back inside. She pulled a couple of fresh sheets from a notebook and tore them into narrow strips. The sound was pleasing, cutting across the silence of the room. In small, neat handwriting, she copied out the poems she wished to keep. Each poem she wound into a scroll, slotting them into the hollow spaces inside the coloured spools. She slid the photograph she loved into a brown paper envelope and placed it at the bottom of the box. She poured coffee into a small china cup, before adding two heaped spoonfuls of dark sugar. Saba returned the tin to the space beneath the sink and stacked the newspapers on top. When the coffee was finished, she poured water over the fire then took herself back to bed, lying fully clothed beneath the yellow cotton sheet.

In the afternoon, a patch of light warmed Saba's cheek and roused her from sleep. The day was luminous, the sun falling in horizontal shafts through the slats of the shutters. She got up, fixed her hair, draped a string of beads around her neck and left the house.

She would not take the bus into town. It was always overcrowded and she would have to stand, the lurch of the potholed roads knocking her bones out of line. Instead, she walked, enjoying the irregular terrain, the dust, the cracks in the dry pavement.

It was a steep climb to the city and the ache of it spread in her calves. The sky was its usual perfect blue; it seemed almost impossible that something so intense could stretch so far. A group of old women passed her. With their bent backs, they looked ancient and fragile, as though they might crumple beneath the weight of their parasols. Teenagers hung together in cliques, meandering along, school books held to their brows to shield their eyes from the sun. Wide suburbs gave way to city streets, dust-covered cars and crowds. Heat and noise swelled, trembling the air.

On a corner of the high street, Saba stopped to catch her breath. Pale yellow plaster from a barber-shop window had flaked away, gathering in a pile beneath the sill. Saba's mind went to the desert, where everything was already turned to dust. Before Mussa left – before he had expressed the wish to leave – she had never given it much thought. From the city's high vantage on the cliff top, it was hard to believe that a world lay beyond it. The escarpment suspended them in cloud and kept them at a heady remove from the outlying land, the sea-bound estu-aries and the coast. As a child, Saba used to like to watch the birds launching from the cliff-edge. They flew out at eye level before dipping suddenly and vanishing into the mist. As for the people here, the thin mountain air had gone to their heads long ago.

She crossed the street, took a side road to her left, another to the right, then swung through the door and into Angelo's. The café was dimly lit, with the blinds drawn low to block the heat. Patches of cool air hung over the glossy red-and-white floor tiles and tickled the sides of her ankles. Her usual table by the window was free and Saba nodded as the waiter gestured her towards it.

In a shadowy corner at the back, Angelo was in his seat. His features were in shadow, but his short white hair shone in the afternoon light. He was reading, making notes. He had not seen her come in and she did not want to disturb him. He would come to her in his own time.

The waiter approached. She ordered coffee and a glass of water, and watched as he pulled the levers on the old Gaggia machine, from which steam hissed and rose. A young mother walked in, her two children in tow. They ran to the counter to press their hands and noses up against the cabinet of cakes and pastries. The mother peeled them away but their fingers, already sticky, left marks on the glass. Saba's coffee arrived and she lifted the cup to her lips without drinking. The mother pointed to two baba cakes, which the waiter handed to her in a brown paper bag, twisted at the corners. Her children snatched it from her and ran towards the door but she did not appear to notice. She was looking, instead, at Angelo.

Angelo had been a friend of Saba's father. She remembered them sitting outside, lighting pipes of cherry-scented tobacco and talking in the dark. Saba used to stand by the door and try to pick out their words from among the noises of the night. They were a nation of poets, her father had once said. If they were not writing, they were reading and listening. Saba remembered Angelo's response, his precise turn of phrase. It is no less essential, he had said, no less nourishing, than blood, than food. Shortly afterwards, Angelo had left and Saba's father had returned inside. He had found Saba sitting on the kitchen floor, writing in the back of one of her school books. She remembered how her hand had moved slowly, methodically, as she concentrated on the formation of each letter in each word.

She was seven years old then, but her father treated her as an adult. He read the four lines she had written with serious eyes then said, quite simply:

'Keep going.'

From that moment on, she made sure that she wrote something every day, forbidding her sisters from disturbing her while she completed the task. He gave her three things: the time to work, the space to think and, on her sixteenth birthday, a writing desk. He had it made to order by a reputable young carpenter in the city, who delivered it in person when the day arrived. Saba remembered Mussa standing at the door – tall and lean with broad shoulders – while her father asked him to join them for coffee and cake. Mussa had talked candidly with her father about how he loved to read, about the importance of writing, and the pleasure it gave him to have been asked to build the desk.

Saba drained her coffee cup, craning back her neck to catch the last drops. She took a pencil and a notebook from her handbag and at the top of a new page wrote: *Desert*, crossed it out, wrote: *Husband*, crossed it out, wrote: *Sand*. She ripped the page out and was about to crumple it in her fist, when she became conscious that Angelo was at her side. He grabbed the paper, pulling it through her fingers and holding it up to the light.

'Mussa's gone?' he said.

Saba nodded.

'He left or he was taken?'

'He left.'

Angelo sat down.

She wished to appear composed, leaning back in her seat and crossing her legs. The muscles in her calves still ached from the walk and, though she knew she must be imagining it, she thought she could feel the badly mended seam weighting down her dress.

'You know you might not hear from him,' Angelo said.

'I know, he'll be in the desert for who knows how long.'

'But after that.'

'What do you mean?'

'I mean you don't know what it will be like.' Angelo leaned across the table and took a sip of her water.

'You mean he'll change.'

Angelo nodded.

'He was already changing,' Saba said.

'Of course he was.'

'I asked him to write to me,' she said.

'And what did he say?'

'That it would be hard.'

Angelo shrugged. 'He won't write.'

They drank two more coffees and a brandy each before leaving the café in the early evening. As they said goodbye, Angelo squeezed Saba's hand and kissed her on the forehead.

The air had cooled. By the time she got home, it was almost dark. There were clusters of stars emerging and a crisp, bright moon. She turned her key in the door, heard the click and swung it open. She reached for the light-switch in the gloom. The open sewing box was on the kitchen table and the edges of the poems that lined the spools were pushing up and out. She sat down and examined the seam she had sewn. The night deepened around her. With a long needle and a pair of sewing scissors, she unpicked her stitches, freeing the pale thread with sharp movements of her hand. The seam gaped like a wound but Saba was suddenly exhausted. She could not face the thought of repairing it again and decided to leave it for the morning.

She replaced the needle in the pin cushion and laid the scissors at the bottom of the box. Where the scrolls were unfurling, she removed them and rolled them into tighter coils.

Saba laid down in bed and waited for sleep. With her eyes open in the dark, she thought of the men in the truck, how it would shake as they drove across the desert into the night. She thought of Mussa moving away from her over the dunes, mapping his journey in her head, imagining his tracks disappearing beneath the next sprinkling of sand carried on the wind.

Number Three

Miss Coral gets up from her desk on a cool October afternoon. She walks over to the kettle and pours steaming liquid into a clear plastic flask, the tea leaves swirling within. Moon is crouched in the corner of the office, a small book of poems on her knees. She learns the lines, breathing out the words.

'Time to go,' says Miss Coral. 'The Director can't catch you here again.' Her tiny frame and button-bright face do not convey the threat she intends. Moon looks up. Her eyes, a little too far apart and as flat and smooth as her forehead, sit open and blank. She gets to her feet. She can't have grown an inch since she got here, Miss Coral thinks.

Number Three

Moon is a scholarship student, transferred from rural Wanzhou. To the Director's surprise, she arrived in Chongqing by train, unaccompanied. She was standing on the platform, carrying her belongings in a bamboo basket strapped to her back with coloured rope. When the Director asked Moon why her parents did not bring her, she replied indirectly. They allowed her to take the train instead of the bus, she said, cutting through the mountains to cross the Golden River in four hours instead of six.

Though Moon has been at Number Three Middle School for two years, she remains the new girl. When she arrived, her grades in Chinese and mathematics were already exceptional, but she had no knowledge of English. Miss Coral was engaged to help her improve until she reached the requisite level for her age. It was felt that once her skill set was complete she would fit in. She never did. One or two of the other students like to mock her country accent; the rest remain aloof. Moon doesn't seem to mind. She neither seeks friendship nor refuses it, and wanders the extensive grounds of the school wearing a look of mild surprise, as though perpetually reliving her first day.

Their English lessons became the first of Miss Coral's extracurricular duties. They met every day at six o'clock in the break between afternoon and evening classes, at the entrance to the school library. They chose always to sit at a table towards the back of the lower ground floor, far away from the computers and the teen-fiction shelves, where few other students gathered. They leant over a new copy of *English Now!*, and Miss Coral made frequent corrections to the textbook's spelling and grammar with corrector fluid and a ballpoint pen. To make time for Moon, Miss Coral had to hand over one of her English literature groups.

A month after their lessons began, rumours started to circulate that the rival school across town had employed a Real English Teacher. Letters from parents of students at Number Three Middle School arrived, threatening the withdrawal of their children. Number Three was supposed to be the best, they said. Why didn't they have such a teacher on their staff? A meeting between the governors and the school's patrons took place and a partnership began with Teach China. Anglophone language teachers would come and go in six-month-long rotations. Miss Coral was charged with the running of the programme. These foreign teachers must receive a good impression of Chinese hospitality, the Director said.

Within a few months of Moon's arrival, Miss Coral

had been removed from the classroom completely. She acquired an office at the end of the Director's corridor from which to conduct her duties as International Hostess. The Director was keen that she should not take the redistribution of her skills as a sign of promotion, so he liked to hint among her colleagues that she had been withdrawn from teaching on grounds of incompetence. It was to be understood that, if it wasn't for his greatness of heart and generosity of spirit, she might not have a job at all.

Miss Coral and Moon moved their evening English lessons from the back of the library to the office. Miss Coral would leave the door open, to save Moon the shame of standing in the corridor like the students awaiting detention. When Miss Coral entered the room she would find Moon hunched over her home-work, sitting squat in the corner with her papers placed neatly in front of her on the floor. At the beginning of each lesson, Miss Coral had to invite Moon to sit down with her at the desk. Moon worked hard, improved quickly, and soon there was no more need for lessons. Yet Miss Coral kept up the habit of leaving her office door open in the evenings, and she would often come back from afternoon meetings with the Director to find Moon in the corner.

'Time to go,' Miss Coral says again. 'I have to be at the airport in an hour.' Moon watches as Miss Coral sips a mouthful of tea and twists the metal cap back onto the flask. She hooks the flask's wire handle over her wrist like an expensive handbag. From the desk, she gathers a small purse, a plastic folder full of papers and a laminated sheet of A4. She slots them into a canvas satchel. Moon makes a small bow towards her, a shimmer of a smile on her lips, then leaves. Less communicative than ever, Miss Coral thinks.

Miss Coral takes a taxi across town. The city is different again. Another skyscraper, another bridge underway; new routes to serve new destinations. The shanty-town shacks of Tianfu, half flattened, are making way for settlement housing. Though she has been here five years, there are moments when life in the city still feels like a shock. In her home town, a few hundred miles into the country, her father is a hospital porter, her mother a department store janitor. She goes to see them twice a year and sends money when she can. Soon a main road will be built connecting the town to the city, and perhaps then things will be different.

The driver winds in and out of the traffic with the front window down, and bursts of cool air flow over

her shoulder as they cross the Jialing. A late afternoon sun casts a haze over the urban sprawl. Smog
and fresh dust linger, hovering over warehouses,
slums and disused factories as they leave the inner
city and approach the airport.

Miss Coral arrives with twenty minutes to spare.
She finds a good spot at the edge of the ribbon that
marks the arrivals gate, takes small sips from her
flask, and waits. When the announcement comes for
the London flight she delves into her satchel and
produces the laminated sheet of A4:

WELCOME TO CHINA
MR JAMES

Amid crowds of Chinese businessmen, a young
white man emerges from the sliding glass doors. He
is tall. His light brown hair is roughed in greasy tufts
and bruise-purple smudges darken the corners of his
eyes. For a moment, he appears lost, then he picks
out Miss Coral's sign from the line-up of hotel taxis
and family reunion balloons. He smiles. Miss Coral
extends her hand towards him as he, simultaneously,
drops into a bow. 'Welcome to Chongqing,' she says,
tapping him stiffly on the arm as he rights himself.

In the taxi on the way back to school, he sleeps.

She watches him, wasting her welcome speech on the driver. *It is an honour to welcome you to China, Mr James. Number Three Middle School is delighted to have a foreign teacher on the staff and, though I know you are yet to begin your teaching career, we are sure that your presence will inspire and encourage the students to improve their language skills and broaden their cultural perspectives.* She stops short of the section where she had intended to explain her role as International Hostess and allows herself, instead, to note the stubble on his neck and chin, and the tear in the left knee of his jeans.

When they arrive, she takes Mr James straight to his apartment on the eleventh floor of the residential building. Only the most senior teachers get their own apartments, the rest bed down six to a room. When she opens the door to his large, unshared space, she expects him to be pleased. He takes a quick look around, runs a palm over the arm of a beige, faux-leather sofa and asks when the flat will be cleaned. She pretends not to have heard this and instead hands over his timetable and a list of codes to the electric school gates. After midnight, she warns, he'll have to call the doorman to let him in. Mr James raises an eyebrow but says nothing. They both sit down. Miss Coral places the six-month contract on the glass-topped coffee table in front of them. It must be signed by tomorrow in order to get the visa ready, she says. With a shrug and a yawn he turns to the back page and crams a string of Latin letters into a space made for three Chinese characters.

A week later, sitting in her office with Moon in the corner, Miss Coral receives a phone call. It is Mr James.

'Hello, Mr James,' she says.

'I need to talk to you,' he begins. 'It's about the money.'

At the mention of money she gets to her feet. Moon looks up from her place.

'So, I've been chatting with my friends,' Mr James continues. 'They're all English teachers. In private foreign-language facilities, mostly. You know, Wall Street English and such. The point is that it seems they're all getting a couple of thousand more than me a month.'

Miss Coral recoils. His words strike her as rude. She states firmly that she would prefer to discuss this in person and asks him to designate a convenient time.

On the way to his flat, she wonders whether or

not to tell him that he's already being paid more than almost all of the other teachers at the school. She considers trying to explain that this is not a private language facility, attended only by the rich children of the city's elite. That Number Three Middle School has too little support for students like Moon. But that would be too patronising, she decides.

When he opens the door, Miss Coral finds the displeasure in his face more violent than she had expected. It seems out of proportion. If she were to ask the Director for a pay rise on his behalf she would be sacked for her audacity on the spot. 'Mr James, I don't have long,' she says. 'Seeing as you already signed the contract I'm afraid there's nothing I can do.'

Mr James opens his mouth to speak but presses his lips together when he sees that she is not finished. She sits down. He joins her.

'Given that this is an ordinary Chinese middle school, and not a supplementary private language facility, there are some perks you may not already be aware of,' she says.

He opens his eyes a little wider, releases some of the tension from his jaw.

'We have a full month off for Chinese New Year

in January,' she says. 'And when the students come back they have two weeks of exams, during which you are not expected to teach.'

'And will I get paid in that time?' says Mr James.

'Yes,' Miss Coral replies. Mr James appears placated and starts musing over the details of a six-week-long trip across South East Asia. Miss Coral, pleasantly surprised by the ease of this negotiation, gets up to leave.

'Look,' he says. She stops and turns her face to his. 'I just can't help but feel it was dishonest, you know, you not telling me I'm getting below average wage.'

'It was written in the contract,' she replies, her eyes smarting at the accusation. His phone, sitting on the coffee table, bleeps loudly. 'And it is not below average,' she says. Mr James taps at the keys of his phone before placing it back on the table. He returns his attention to the room. There is a silence.

'Look,' Mr James says again, studying her face with intent. Miss Coral notices that his eyes rest a moment on her lips. 'I don't want to fall out in my first week.'

When she gets back to her office, Miss Coral finds that Moon is still there, squatting birdlike in the corner. The small of her back is flat against the wall, heels off the floor, with her weight on the balls of her feet. As usual, she has a book perched on her knees. As Miss Coral arranges herself at the desk, Moon gets up, scattering loose tea into the flask. A rush of hissing water hits the bottom of the plastic cup and Miss Coral watches as it fills.

At the beginning of November, Mr James calls Miss Coral to ask if she would like to go to dinner with his friends. Show us your favourite haunt, he suggests. She meets them by the school gates. Mr James is there with two blonde girls – Sybil, who is French, and Carey, an American – and three unshaven young men who introduce themselves as Johnny, Kit and Max, leaving their nationalities undisclosed. Miss Coral takes them to the best Fire Pot restaurant in Shapingba. The menu comes on a clipboard: it is a checklist of items grouped into vegetables, meat and side dishes. They all turn to face Miss Coral.

'How spicy do you like it?' she says, placing ticks and numbers beside a dozen or more items on the menu.

A cauldron of red broth arrives: a ferocious-looking concoction of sesame oil, fresh chillies and Sichuan peppercorns. Two waiters hold it while the centre circle of the table is removed and a gas canister placed beneath. The gunmetal cauldron is placed in the hole in the middle of the table and the flame from the gas brings bubbles, thick and slow, to the surface of the soup. Skewered ingredients appear on platters: cloud ear mushrooms, winter melon, lotus root and pak choi. Miss Coral shows them how long to cook each one, plunging her chopsticks into the soup and deftly removing chilli-soaked hunks of blood-red pumpkin and yam.

Empty bottles of beer gather beneath the table. *Pi jiu* seems to be the only Chinese word they know and they order in bulk, making hashed attempts at the Mandarin. She tries to teach them Chinese finger spelling for numbers, mapping the shapes of the characters with her hands.

For most of the evening, Miss Coral says little and busies herself sharing out food from the pot. She listens as they compare culture shocks – *Why is everyone always shouting?* – *Someone touched my hair on the bus* – *I'd give anything for a cheese and pickle sandwich* – *Make mine a PB and J.* Miss Coral is surprised to find how much she enjoys hearing the critique. No one asks those kinds of questions in Chinese. The French girl, Sybil, is sitting on her right. As another round of beer is ordered, Sybil leans towards her. She speaks softly. 'Do you like living in China?' she says.

'I've never lived anywhere else,' says Miss Coral.

'Don't you want to travel?'

Miss Coral says she has no plans to do so. Before she can elaborate, the French girl asks her what she does in her spare time.

'I like translating things,' she says, after a pause. 'And perhaps that's as good as travelling. Perhaps it's better. No jet lag,' she says. As she speaks she addresses the simmering broth. An old university professor still sends her bits of translation work, she says, but she can't tell the Director, or anyone at Number Three Middle School. On a whim, last year, she applied to do a Masters in Translation in Beijing. She got accepted, but she can't take up her place. Miss Coral laughs at herself. She has a good job, she says, thinking of the teaching she once loved. When she looks up at Sybil, Miss Coral sees that she is no longer listening, is paying more attention to balancing domed mouthfuls of rice on her chopsticks.

The end of the evening comes. Miss Coral and Mr James share a taxi back to the school. The night guards open the gate and Miss Coral gives them a tip. They walk up the wide avenue towards the residential building, then they ride the lift together. When it stops at his floor, Mr James says goodnight, stopping the doors with his foot. He leans over and kisses Miss Coral on the cheek. She smells the beer on his breath.

'Fuck,' he says, 'I forgot you don't kiss in China.' He walks into the dimly-lit hallway, laughing to himself.

Miss Coral takes the lift up to the twelfth floor. She tries not to wake her roommates as she slips into bed, fully dressed, listening to the sound of the other teachers breathing in their sleep.

December proves troublesome. One afternoon, Mr James comes to her office. A student is causing him concern and he has come to ask that something be done; he thinks perhaps the boy has Down's syndrome. Miss Coral does not recognise the phrase and asks Mr James to write it down. After he has gone, she looks the words up, and is confused by myriad translations in Chinese. She arranges to observe the class in question the next day, during their history lesson. She takes care to pick a slot in the timetable when she knows that Mr James will be busy teaching other classes.

Miss Coral immediately picks out the student

concerned. He is a large boy, unusually tall, and is sitting at the back of the room. He swings on his chair, writes nothing down, and is ignored by his classmates and history teacher alike. When a stream of incomprehensible noises escape his lips, the history teacher turns and gives a sharp reprimand in Mandarin, silencing the boy. Mr James, of course, can only discipline in English, and perhaps this is the problem.

Miss Coral speaks to the Director, who presents a simple solution. The boy can be removed from Mr James' lessons as soon as he causes trouble. The director gives Miss Coral a key to a cupboard in an adjacent corridor where the boy can sit until English is over. It would be prudent to lock him in, the Director says.

When Mr James is next scheduled to take the class, Miss Coral waits for him to arrive outside their classroom. In her careful English, she explains the lesson she observed and the Director's advice, and hands over the key. Mr James stares at her. Miss Coral is aware of the muscles in his mouth tightening. He looks towards the classroom door then brings his eyes back to meet hers: 'I'd rather he screamed for an hour than lock him up in a cupboard. That's fucking disgusting,' he says. Mr James enters the classroom, slamming the door behind him.

It is not until she is back in her office that Miss Coral allows herself to cry. When Moon opens the door, she lingers a moment on the threshold. She takes up her usual position in the corner and keeps her head down as Miss Coral pats her cheeks dry and smoothes the front of her shirt. When Miss Coral has straightened herself Moon still does not look up. She has her head dipped over her book, tracing the lines with her finger and making occasional notes in the margins. For the first time, Miss Coral is aware of the calming presence Moon exerts on the room. Miss Coral gets up and leaves. When she returns, she is holding a small wooden stool and a cushion.

'Stand up, Moon,' she says, and Moon obeys. She places the stool and cushion in the corner and Moon smiles in a way that Miss Coral has not seen before. It feels as though the sun has moved a little closer to their window.

Towards the middle of the month, Mr James demands a Christmas holiday. The Director allows him the twenty-fifth and twenty-sixth. He pushes for the twenty-fourth. Miss Coral, receiving his urgent text messages and voicemails, is too afraid to ask for more. When she plucks up the courage to approach the Director again, it takes less than a second for him to refuse her. When Mr James phones in sick on 24 December, instead of docking his pay cheque the Director docks hers. Everyone will know, she thinks. That night, Miss Coral makes sure she is in bed, feigning sleep, long before her roommates arrive.

In January, Mr James leaves for Vietnam – 'a six-week romp down the East Coast, Halong Bay, Nha Trang and Ho Chi Fucking Minh', as he puts it to her in an email. Miss Coral returns to her hometown for Chinese New Year. By the time she leaves, the school is almost empty. She has been working hard on her latest translations, making the most of the office. Moon, too, has stayed behind, helping where she can, making creative suggestions. They share a taxi to the train station before embarking on long cross-country journeys in opposite directions.

Two weeks later, when Miss Coral comes back to school, she finds a postcard from Mr James on her desk. Halong Bay. He gives her the date of his return. He will miss the start of term, he says, *because the flights are too expensive*. She breaks the news to the Director by email. He informs Miss Coral that she will have to cover the classes and that Mr James' wages will be docked by a quarter.

Nervously, Miss Coral paraphrases the Director's response into an email for Mr James, to which she receives no reply. When she next hears from him, he is already back in China, and has other things on his mind.

In his absence, his apartment had become home to a swarm of flying ants. He arrived to find the floor carpeted with insect corpses and the air about him thick with the survivors. *What,* his email said, *is the school going to do about this?*

On the third day of term, Miss Coral is already exhausted. What does he want her to do? Go over there and sweep up the insects herself? She writes back, conveying her sympathies but making it clear that the maintenance of his apartment does not come under her job description. She recommends that he buy insect spray and offers to hire a cleaner on his behalf, though he will have to pay. Beyond that, she is powerless. Miss Coral clicks 'Send' and finds that her head is filled with images of ants raining from ceiling to floor. They are flooding the room like the sand of an egg timer.

When Mr James's contract comes to an end on 31 March, Miss Coral throws him a farewell party. She flits between classrooms, brandishing a basketball shirt bearing the school logo on which students paint parting wishes and well-worn quotations in permanent fabric marker. Everybody writes something. Across the left shoulder blade, Moon writes a line from Confucius, with a translation in brackets: 'Wheresoever you go, go with all your heart.'

In a large classroom on the second floor, they convene. Some groups of girls have prepared traditional Chinese songs to sing. Others come laden with white cardboard boxes containing sticky piles of egg custard pastries and sanguine jujube dates. Black-and-white sachets of White Rabbit Candy garnish the tables and bottles of sweet jasmine tea line the window sills. Mr James appears genuinely moved. Miss Coral hands him a card she made herself, done in traditional Chinese calligraphy. Inside the card, her message conveys her thanks, on behalf of Number Three Middle School, for his freeness of spirit and passion for equality. *It is of utmost importance*, she writes, *for Chinese students to speak good English, so that they may have more colourful opportunities in their futures.*

When he gets back to England, Mr James sends her an email returning her thanks. She opens it from the office computer. He will never forget such a pretty little face, he says, and Miss Coral puts her hands to her cheeks to mask the flush she feels rising as she reads.

Number Three

In early April, Miss Coral is called to the Director's office. A letter has come from Teach China, from their Chinese delegate in Chongqing. He hands it across to Miss Coral and demands that she read it aloud.

To the Director of Number Three Middle School,

Following a letter of complaint, demanding considerable compensation, we must express to you the concerns of our client. Mr James reported to us that he was dissatisfied with his rate of pay. Furthermore, he was somewhat disappointed by the arrangements for the Christmas holidays. (Christmas, we would like to remind you, is one of the most important events in the Western calendar.) The accommodation provided was less than satisfactory, a statement for which he provided photographic evidence. In dealing with these matters, Mr James claimed that he felt underrepresented at the school, being unable, himself, to communicate with the authorities in Mandarin.

'That will do,' says the Director.
Miss Coral feels something like a stone lodge in her throat. She prays she won't be asked any

questions. Her mouth is too dry, her throat too small for speech.

'I'm sure you know what this means,' the Director goes on. 'You will be paid for the rest of the month, but we ask that you leave today.'

It takes less than thirty minutes for Miss Coral to pack her belongings into a large canvas rucksack. She peels the sheets from the bed and folds them neatly into a pile. She lingers for as long as she can in the office, reorganising paperwork and deleting old emails. When the door clicks open, she flinches, but when she looks up there is no one standing in the doorway.

She pulls a piece of paper from the notebook in her handbag and tries to think of what she might say to Moon. But even if she could find the words, she decides, where would she put the note? And how could she possibly know that Moon would be the one to find it? She folds up the paper and slots it back into the notebook.

When the office is clean and bare, Miss Coral opens the window to refresh the air. She places the clear plastic flask and an unopened packet of tea leaves beneath Moon's stool in the corner. As she leaves she lets the office door swing wide.

In the taxi across town, through the smog and the

Number Three

half-hearted spring rain, Miss Coral has time to note that the Tianfu slums have now been flattened completely.

Nemeral

Ruby span, around and around, in a tomato-red coat and yellow wellies and with her arms outstretched, like a brightly painted spinning top. She was humming; buzzing like a bee, or a dragonfly, at times almost breaking into song. Ellen stood near her sister, watching. Ellen was older, too old for this kind of thing. She had always been too old to be much of a child, but Ruby – Ruby was a whirlwind.

Ruby kept on spinning and began to flap her arms up and down, like some kind of magical bird.

'Fly!' she said, spinning faster.

'Fly where?' said Ellen.

'I don't care!' Ruby squealed. 'I don't care!'

❧

Sophie locked the car and they walked together to the parking attendant. She hadn't wanted to leave them alone in the car alone, even for a minute. She took her responsibilities very seriously. They frightened and exhilarated her at once.

It was two o'clock. Sophie paid for four hours, though they would only need three; they would leave at five, for them to eat at five thirty, which would leave enough time for stories, teeth brushing and bedtime hair-plaiting, before Victoria came home. The attendant gave her a map and a voucher for ice cream. He pointed at a drab little stall by the entrance gate, a picture of a strawberry cone on the side. 'Shuts at five,' he said.

'I want chocolate. Will he have chocolate?' Ellen asked the attendant, looking up at him and squinting, one eye closed.

'Should do,' he said, more friendly. 'What about you?' He was looking at Ruby.

'I'll have vanilla with dolly mixtures' said Ruby. 'That's my favourite.'

'Very particular,' said the attendant, looking at Sophie, who smiled and led them back to the car.

'Remember you're on the south side,' he called after them. Then he said something else, more quietly, that might have been 'which is never on the north' or 'which is ever on and off' or 'witches live in the north', none of which made any sense.

Middle afternoon. The shadows of tree spines were lengthening and bright squares of warm light flashed across the girls' heads and shoulders where the sun was breaking through the branches. Sophie had come here with her father, before he left and before he died, which were different things, different in ways that Sophie was still untangling. But she remembered her father with a map and a compass and the pleasure he took in navigating his way around what, Sophie now saw, was a clearly sign-posted trail. She understood: it was the sense of adventure, of doing it for yourself. That said, the forest wasn't quite as she remembered it. There was a cycling trail marked in yellow, along which families trundled; little ones with stabilisers, the littlest ones in baby seats, asleep. There were joggers in neon jackets. People with prams.

The trail was a two-hour walk, but Sophie only wanted to do part of it, in case the girls got tired or hungry. She wasn't sure if this was the kind of thing they liked. Sophie looked at the map. The trails on the paper didn't appear to match the directions indicated on the signpost beside them. Sophie had thought there was a compass on her phone but she couldn't find it, and anyway there was no signal. Would the compass work without signal? Did it matter when there were so many people? So many signposts?

'Well, we can go this way, or this way,' she said to the girls, immediately regretting giving them the choice.

'This way!' Ruby said, pointing towards a gap in the trees, away from the marked route.

'Is that all right with you, Ellen?'

'Why that way, Ruby?' said Ellen.

'I saw a squirrel.'

'You did not.'

'I did too.'

'So shall we go this way?' said Sophie.

'Yes, this way,' said Ellen.

They left the path.

❧

They had reached a clearing when Ruby ran to Sophie's side and pulled on the cuff of her coat sleeve.

'Can we draw?' said Ruby.

'You hate drawing,' said Ellen, hanging back.

'I do not. Actually' – she pronounced this very

slowly, ack-chew-alley – 'I used to hate drawing. Now I really like it. A lot.'

Ellen rolled her eyes and looked at Sophie.

'Did you pack the things, Ellen?' said Sophie.

Ellen nodded.

Sophie slid the backpack off her shoulders and the girls dived in, foraging for paper and pens, pulling out juice cartons, bananas, a variety of match-box-sized snacks.

'I was sure you didn't like drawing,' Ellen muttered. 'You didn't like it yesterday.'

Ruby said nothing.

They took a sketchpad each and Sophie held up the colouring pencils in a fist and told them to choose.

'The green isn't green enough,' said Ruby, looking at the trees. 'You need a green that's green like a nemeral.'

'A nemeral?' said Sophie.

'Like a ruby, but green,' said Ruby.

'I'll take the green one,' said Ellen.

'What do you want, Ruby?' said Sophie.

'I don't care!' said Ruby, then, solemnly, 'Black, please.'

The two girls crouched on the forest floor with the sketchpads on their knees. A cloud drifted over the sun. Looking about her, she saw the forest was not so tame. Above them were tangled branches. Sophie focused on the blackest thing she could find.

Eventually, she took another sketchpad from the rucksack, and a grey pencil crayon, and started to draw. Ellen looked up.

'Do you want the green, Sophie?'

'I'm OK, thanks, Ellen, but you're kind to ask.'

That was the last thing anyone said for a time. They drew with the sounds of the forest around them – things crunching, rustling; an occasional squeak; perhaps, quite far away, the sound of water. Drawing made Sophie feel smaller. Not childlike exactly, but less important somehow.

They drew until Ellen said that she absolutely could not crouch on the floor any longer. There was a cramp in her leg and she had to shake it out.

'Are you finished, Ruby?' said Ellen, hopping about and kicking the air.

Ruby placed a final, exuberant stroke on her sketchpad. 'Finished!' she said.

'Let's see.'

Ellen examined the drawing carefully and remarked that Ruby's leaves were very nicely drawn, if a little too large. Then she pointed to a squiggly form at the bottom of the page. It was mostly knots and spirals but there were also eyes and the possibility of a tail. 'What's that?' said Ellen.

'A squirrel,' said Ruby.

'You never saw a squirrel. You would've said.'

'I made it up!' said Ruby. 'Made-up squirrel.'

Sophie walked over to look.

'Nice squirrel,' she said. Ruby did a little squirrel dance, hopping and waving her drawing around in the air.

The girls handed their drawing materials to Sophie, who packed them away in the rucksack and gave them each a carton of juice. They sucked noisily through their straws as they walked.

'Mum makes us sit down to drink,' said Ellen, and Sophie wondered if she had broken some grievous rule – if they were in danger of choking, or of spilling juice on their new, clean coats.

After a few paces, beneath a small patch of light, Sophie heard her phone bleep. She took it out of her pocket but her hands were cold, far colder than she had thought, and the phone slipped to the forest floor, hitting rock not earth. It made a hard, loud noise and skidded away. Before Sophie could move, Ellen skipped over and picked it up, cupping it anxiously in two hands, as though it were sand or water. 'It's cracked,' she said, holding it up for Sophie to see. Sophie took the phone from Ellen and their eyes met. Ellen looked frightened, as though she might cry. Sophie took the phone in both hands, as

Ellen had. Through the constellation of cracked glass, she read the message. It was from Victoria. *Hope you're all having a super time and they're being good . . . Keep safe.*

Sophie liked Victoria, more than her mother did, although Victoria was her mother's friend. Victoria was glamorous and colourful. She had a careless kind of confidence that Sophie admired. She did her face in public and could apply red lipstick without a mirror. Sophie's mother was stricter, she laughed more quietly and only wore the kind of make-up you couldn't see. She said that Victoria was posh, and occasionally used the word 'pretentious', which Sophie thought was unfair. But she knew that in high school her father had been Victoria's friend, too, that perhaps there had been a fling, or a date, or a party, or something, and she knew better than to contradict her mother.

But whatever her mother might say about Victoria, they were loyal to one another. When Sophie's father had left – in the night, no note, not a phone call for weeks, until, one day, the announcement in the post that he had moved to Connecticut, USA, and that he was not coming back – Victoria had taken the two of them under her exuberant wing. She loved women, she said, and hated men, even hated her husband sometimes. Women, she said, were the creatures of God – or was it the devil? Creatures of magic, witchery and mystic power.

Then, when her father had died – hit by a drunk-driver while walking down the pavement – and Sophie and her mother were left to untangle the two different forms of abandonment they faced, Victoria had been there, too. At first, she cooked and cleaned, bringing Ellen and Ruby with her while she worked. Then, once the initial shock had passed, she helped Sophie's mother to take her first trips out of the house. That was when Sophie began to babysit the girls. At first, she had been a little afraid of them and the responsibilities they brought, but they quickly won her over and she won them right back.

And now there was love, between the five of them, in all directions.

❧

Sophie ran a finger along the crack splitting the screen. Ellen stood by her side.

'Ruby broke Papa's phone, once. That was bad,' she said.

'Where is Ruby?' said Sophie, turning around and shoving the phone back in her pocket. 'Ruby!'

No answer.

'Ruby!'

'Here!' said Ruby, from some trees, perhaps fifteen feet from where they stood. 'I found a leaf-hill!'

'A what?'

'Where are you, Ruby? Where are you actually?' said Ellen. Then to Sophie: 'Look for her boots. They're extremely yellow.'

Ellen and Sophie crouched together, peering exaggeratedly through thickets of spindly, black trees looking for a flash of yellow rubber boot. Ellen spotted it first, and they ran, but the boots disappeared, and Ruby was screaming.

Sophie and Ellen ran in the direction of yellow and reached the top of a steep slope. It went down some fifty feet, a sharp dip, like a sinkhole filled with leaves. At the bottom was Ruby, spinning, kicking leaves into the air around her, happy as pie.

'What are you doing down there?' Sophie shouted.

'Just spinning.'

'How did you get down?' said Ellen. 'It looks a long way.'

'Sausage-roly-poly.'

'Oh, for goodness' sake,' said Ellen, looking at Sophie.

'Can you get back up?' Sophie shouted.

Ruby was still. She looked up at them, thinking hard. 'I can't get back up,' she said in a serious voice.

She looked at them. They looked at her. 'I just can't get back up,' said Ruby, again. 'Roly-poly doesn't work that way round.' She started to cry.

'It's OK, Ruby,' said Sophie. 'I'll come down.'

'What about me?' said Ellen.

'You wait here. It's steep,' said Sophie.

'I'd rather come,' said Ellen. 'I don't want to be left alone.'

'Right then.' Sophie took a deep breath. She would rather leave her at the top – there were so many slipping hazards – but now Ellen had said what she had said she felt it would be asking for trouble to do so. She crouched at the edge of the slope and placed her hands on the cold, leaf-covered ground. 'It's cold, but it's not wet,' she said to Ellen. They shuffled down the slope on their bottoms, leaves sticking to their hands, slipping when they lost their grip.

'We're coming, Ruby, we'll be there soon,' Sophie said. Ruby was drying her eyes. She watched them come all the way down, standing very still. When they reached her, at the centre of the pit, they wrapped her up in a big hug.

'You're so annoying,' said Ellen, under her breath, and Ruby sobbed into her sister's coat. When she dried her eyes, Ruby said: 'Roly-poly was quicker,' but then she was quiet.

Sophie had a bad feeling about this. It had been much harder to get down than she had thought. She looked about to find the easiest way back up to the forest floor. It seemed perhaps the slope was not quite so steep on the far side, but it would take them a long way from the trail.

'My hand is hurting,' said Ellen.

Sophie looked but couldn't see anything. Then a red patch formed across the squidgy bit of her palm.

'How does it hurt? Like a stinging-nettle hurts?' said Sophie.

'No, like a bruise hurts,' said Ellen. 'Achy.'

'What if I touch it?' Sophie brushed a fingertip along Ellen's outstretched hand.

Ellen flinched: 'Hurts more!' she said. As Sophie examined Ellen's hand, the patch got redder and a rash formed. It was bumpy, spotted.

'You're sure it wasn't a nettle?' Sophie said.

'It wasn't a nettle,' said Ellen. 'It's a different kind of hurt.'

Sophie looked in the bag to see what she had packed.

'Savlon?' she said.

Ellen shook her head.

'Plaster?'

Ellen shook her head again.

74

'How about some magic, then?' said Sophie.

Ellen grinned. Ruby wrapped her arms round Sophie's leg.

'Follow me,' she said to Ruby. 'Do as I do.' Sophie raised her arms above her head. Looking up, the forest was impossibly bright and impossibly dark all at once. Black leaves and pillars of late-afternoon sun. They waved their arms up and down several times, as though worshipping Ellen's hand. Sophie twirled, Ruby twirled.

'Fly!' said Ruby. They twirled faster. Sophie's head began to hurt. She stood and turned to face Ellen.

'How's that?' she said, pointing to Ellen's hand.

Ellen smiled. 'Better!'

'Really?' said Sophie.

'Not totally,' said Ellen, 'but better.'

Sophie looked at Ellen's hand. It did indeed look better. Some of the redness had gone. A cloud drew overhead. The darkening sky reminded Sophie that they should think about getting back to the path.

'I'm tired,' said Ruby.

'I'm hungry,' said Ellen.

Sophie took a couple of packets of raisins and a chocolate bar from the rucksack and they shared out the goods. While the girls ate, Sophie explored their options. It was true that the slope was gentler on the far side, but parts of it were still steep and the ground was rockier: it would hurt them if they fell. She looked back at the way they had come. From this angle, it seemed impossible that they had made it down at all, and a miracle that Ruby had not been hurt, hit her head on something, twisted a wrist or an ankle. It was time to be serious, Sophie thought; time to stop pretending she was still a little girl.

They made their way up the far side of the dip. It was hard work, dead leaves slipping against the soles of their shoes, dry earth loosening. Every thirty-odd seconds Ruby sighed, loudly, to let everyone know what a hard time she was having. She puffed out her little red cheeks with the exertion and appeared to have forgotten that this was all her doing. Ellen got on with it quietly, but Sophie could hear she was out of breath and Sophie, too, was finding the climb rather tricky. At one point, Ellen grazed a knuckle and asked Sophie to magic it better.

'When we get to the top,' said Sophie, and Ellen looked up.

'But that's ages away,' Ellen said. 'By then it will be dark.'

It was true that the light had dimmed, but Sophie thought it was just the clouds, or the thickening branches overhead. But perhaps Ellen was right. Sophie checked her phone. It was half past four. She tried to remember what time it had been getting dark recently. Around six, she thought. Perhaps half past. Sophie tried to work out how long it would take to get back to the trail. She thought she knew which direction to take.

When they were back at the level of the forest floor, all three breathing hard, Sophie realised that the other people that had seemed so annoying earlier – the cyclists, joggers and families – were no longer there.

❧

The fading light had the curious effect of making everything sharper; brighter, even, in its new definition.

'What are we doing now, Sophie?' said Ruby. They had been walking for some time, in the direction Sophie had thought would lead them back to the trail, but they hadn't found it.

'Well,' said Sophie, playfully, 'I just thought we could stay here, actually. Build a camp fire. Craft three swords out of wood and prepare to fight the forest monsters.'

'Forest monsters?' said Ellen. 'Shouldn't we go home and have dinner? We always have dinner at half past five. And it's Thursday. Fish fingers.'

'I hate fish fingers,' said Ruby.

Ellen rolled her eyes,

'I hate fish fingers,' said Ruby again. 'Let's stay here!'

'We could make a forest dinner,' said Sophie. 'We could forage for berries and make squirrel sandwiches.'

'Squirrel sandwiches!' said Ruby. She pretended to throw up on the grass.

'Oh, but so nutritious,' said Sophie. 'Lots of protein, to make your fur nice and shiny.'

'Can you really eat squirrels?' said Ellen.

'I'm sure you could, if you were really hungry.'

'So why don't we eat them?' said Ellen.

'I suppose because we have other things to eat. Like fish fingers.'

'Do you know where we are?' said Ellen, suddenly serious.

Sophie tried very hard to look calm, to be the grown-up.

Sophie took her cracked phone out of the pocket. There was no signal but the compass seemed to work nonetheless. Sophie found south, to take them in the direction of the car park.

'We just walk in a straight line,' said Sophie, 'To the edge of the forest, and then we walk around the forest to the car park. Ellen, you can be in charge of the compass.'

She took Ruby's hand and Ruby took Ellen's and they walked. No one spoke.

Sophie was worried. What if the direction was wrong? If they walked for hours and hours without finding a path or a sign? If they didn't get back before Victoria? This was more like the forest she remembered being in as a girl with her father. Except that then it was fun to be afraid, because with him, she had thought, she was safe. It was manageable; he had managed it. Someone else was in charge. It was not so fun to be afraid when you were the one leading the troops. Were there forest rangers? Would someone find them at this hour? She thought of the temporary shelters they might build, the flames of the imaginary camp fire and the sounds of deep, deep night. She tried to tell herself that perhaps they had entered a particularly dense patch of trees; that the clouds were thickening; that there was a storm. But Sophie knew it was dark, and that night had begun.

They walked in a straight line with Ellen checking the compass on the phone. The signal came and went but the compass appeared to stay true – a kind of magic Sophie didn't understand. Ruby was in good spirits, telling stories about the children she was friends with at playschool, who seemed to inter-mingle with characters she had seen in films or heard about in books read to her. Neither Sophie nor Ellen were listening carefully. Ellen was concentrating hard on the compass, a little giddy with the responsibility she had been given, and Sophie was trying to see through the darkness to make out any clearings, pathways or tree clusters that she might recognise from her childhood. Every few minutes, she checked her watch. It seemed to be taking a long time for them to get anywhere. That they had not yet reached the forest's outer limit made Sophie wonder if they were headed in the wrong direction.

'What's the time, Sophie?' asked Ruby.

Sophie paused, wondering whether or not to lie. 'It's half past five,' she said, truthfully.

Ellen took an exaggerated, cartoon-style gasp of air. 'But we have dinner at half past five,' she said. 'And we're not even home! We're not even in the car!'

'I know,' said Sophie, 'but that's sometimes what happens when you have an adventure. Things get out of sync.'

'Things like fish fingers?' said Ruby.

'Yes, exactly.'

At the mention of food, they were hungry, so they stopped to get the last of the snacks from her bag. Sophie thought she had overpacked but they had stayed so late that only two packs of raisins, a satsuma and one carton of blackcurrant juice remained.

While the girls were busy with their snacks Sophie took the light from the phone and shone it around them. The clearing in which they stood looked familiar, somehow. She had a feeling that perhaps they had passed through it earlier in the afternoon, which would mean they must have looped back on themselves, and that they had not been going straight after all.

Ellen scrunched up the empty cereal-bar wrappers and shoved them to the bottom of the rucksack.

'Same direction as before?' she said, retrieving the phone and finding the compass. She was excitable, high on the spirit of adventure.

'That's the one!' said Sophie, in as bright and sure-sounding a voice as she could manage.

They came to a tall wire fence. Sophie brushed it with a fingertip. It was not electric. She and Ellen climbed through the large gap between the two middle wires. Ruby threw herself flat on the ground and sausage-rolled her way out. She jumped to her feet, looking pleased with herself for a moment, before becoming sad.

'What is it, Ruby?' said Sophie.

Ruby said nothing but held on to Sophie's leg.

They were standing on the wide verge of a main road, though there was not much traffic. It ought to have felt safer, being out of the forest, but Sophie felt exposed. The few cars that passed did so at great speed. She took the crumpled map from her pocket and found their position. They would have to walk another half an hour, skirting the forest's edge, before they reached the car park. It was a quarter past six. Victoria would be back around seven. There wouldn't be time to have them fed and washed before then. But the most important thing, Sophie reminded herself, was to make sure they all got home safely.

'Come on,' she said. Only a handful of cars passed them as they went. Each time one came, Sophie watched the glare of the headlights cast three long shadows out in front of them. She held their hands tightly, lest they run out into the road. As the cars sped on, the shadows were flung across the wire fence and into the forest before vanishing completely.

At the car park, hers was the only car remaining. She checked her wipers for a ticket but there was only a flyer for a charity run, which she shoved in her pocket.

'Can we have ice cream?' said Ellen.

Sophie felt bad. She had promised, but if the stall was closed there was nothing she could do. 'Next time,' she said.

Sophie and Ellen pulled the leaves off Ruby's coat and out of her hair. Something shiny and bright was stuck to her sock.

'Here,' said Ellen, handing it to Sophie and shining the phone towards it. It was a necklace, one of those Friends-Forever things, with half a heart and a chain, and a little green stone in the middle.

'A nemeral, Ruby, look,' said Sophie, and Ruby nodded.

'Can I keep it?' said Ellen.

'No,' said Sophie. 'We should just leave it here.'

'But it's lost. No one will find it.'

'Yes but—'

'If I kept it, I could take it to the police.'

'I don't think someone would go to the police over a necklace like this,' said Sophie.

'But you said it was an *emerald*,' said Ellen. 'You said,' Ellen repeated. 'I heard you.'

'Yes, but it's probably not a real one,' said Sophie,

who didn't quite know why this whole business with the necklace was bothering her so much.

'We could take it back to the fence!' said Ellen, starting to walk. 'So the forest people will find it!'

'Ellen!'

Ellen did not turn around.

'Ellen, you come back here right this instant.'

Ruby reached for Sophie's hand. She started to cry. 'I don't want to go back to the dark,' said Ruby. Ellen stopped where she was but did not turn to face them.

'We're not going back to the dark,' Sophie said to Ruby. 'But we're going to bring your sister back to the car.'

Sophie and Ruby walked to meet Ellen where she was standing stock still. When they reached her, Ellen was crying very quietly.

'It's just . . .' Ellen began, 'If I had a necklace like this, I'd be very upset if I lost it.' She sobbed again. 'And it is really very difficult to know what to do.'

Sophie and Ruby wrapped themselves around Ellen in a hug.

'Give it to me, Ellen.'

Ellen handed over the necklace. Sophie thought about what to do. It had become important. She felt a strange urge to bury it, as though it might one day become a clue in some story, a secret between her and someone else.

Finally, she said: 'We could hang it up on a branch, near the entrance. Then if someone comes to find it, they'll see it quickly.'

Ellen thought about this a moment. 'OK,' she said. They all walked towards the entrance and hung the necklace on a low branch, where it glinted against the light from the road. They stood, holding hands, in reverence.

❧

Ellen sat in the front of the car and Ruby nodded off in the back. Sophie listened to the radio at low volume and Ellen talked about how she was much too old to be doing the potato-print painting her class was busy with at school, but how she quite liked it anyway.

'What are you painting?' asked Sophie.

'Autumn leaves, but it's taken so long to mix all the different shades of brown it's almost winter now, and we still haven't finished.'

The local radio seemed only to play advertisements and Sophie tried to change the station but all she could find was white noise. She turned it off.

'Were you scared when we got lost?' said Ellen.

'Not really.'

'I thought maybe the necklace belonged to someone who'd got lost.'

'Like who?'

'Just someone like me or you. But who didn't find their way back.'

'Or maybe someone just lost a necklace. Dropped it or something,' said Sophie. 'What are you reading at the moment, Ellen?'

Ellen was good at reading and liked to talk about it. Her current book was about a coven of witches – some who were friends, some who were cousins and sisters – who made magic for good and for bad and sometimes got into trouble. The main character was a young woman, learning grown-up magic and getting it wrong. Ellen started at the beginning of the story and made a winding rehash of the plot. Sophie continued to think on the darkness of the forest.

'And in my head she looks like you, Sophie,' said Ellen.

'Who looks like me?'

'The young witch, the main one, the one growing up and getting her spells mixed up.'

'Why me?' said Sophie.

'Because she sounds like she would be very pretty. And I like her a lot,' said Ellen.

Sophie smiled and remembered it was too dark

for Ellen to see that she was smiling. 'Thank you,' she said.

'Sophie,' said Ellen, 'I wish I was a witch.'

'Me too,' said Sophie. The rest of the way home they were quiet.

❧

By the time they got back, nobody wanted fish fingers. Sophie made them toast and honey and the girls got into their pyjamas, brushed their teeth and climbed into bed: Ruby first, then Ellen. Because Ellen was so good at reading now, she liked to be the one to read Ruby her bedtime story. While Ellen read – something about a dog and a lost shoe – Sophie still couldn't get her mind away from the forest. They were safe, the girls were at home, Victoria would be back any minute, yet something felt frightening, still. What would it have been like, Sophie wondered, to stay there overnight, to wake in the morning and wonder at their survival? A whole other country. A singing in the trees, that aching noise that forests make; two children, wild and free, skipping and screaming; magical creatures; a witch in the woods, looking for a necklace with a nemeral, wandering aimlessly in that vast and dangerous garden.

❧

By the time Ellen got into bed, she was too tired to read to herself, so Sophie read her a few pages from her witch book but before long Ellen's eyes were closing. Sophie put the book down.

'Are you ready to sleep, now?' Sophie asked.

Ellen ignored the question.

'What are you going to do, Sophie?' said Ellen. 'Now that you don't have to go to school.'

'I don't know,' said Sophie. 'I have to think for a while.'

'You should be an explorer,' said Ellen.

'You should be going to sleep,' said Sophie.

'You should be an explorer and you should explore every country in the world.'

'If you say so,' said Sophie.

'You'd have all kinds of adventures and you'd never be scared because you're so brave.'

'Is that right?' said Sophie.

'Or you might be scared, sometimes, but you'd still be brave enough.'

'Well, I'm glad you think so.'

'But take care, now, Sophie,' said Ellen, closing her eyes and sounding just like Victoria. 'You just take extremely good care.'

The Professor

Smoke was twisting its way into Ruth's dream, making her sister's face, which had been floating in and out of focus, cloud over. There was the sound of coughing and Ruth was trying to speak, to ask her sister if she was all right, when she woke up and understood that the coughing she had heard was, in fact, her own. The dream vanished and Ruth ran to the bedroom window and saw that the apartment block on the other side of the street was ablaze. Clouds of dark smoke rose up from it, the glow of the fire still bright within. Behind frames of shattered glass, large wooden beams glimmered and fell and ceilings appeared to melt.

Ruth blinked. She thought about opening the window, but didn't.

There was a knock at the door. Ruth ran to answer it. Before she could say hello, a firefighter was telling her to leave.

It was the end of November and already near freezing. Ruth pulled her coat from the row of hooks in the narrow hallway. She only just remembered to pocket her key before following the fireman out onto the landing. She pointed at the professor's door, which stood directly opposite the door to her sister's apartment, and the fireman told her that the old lady was already outside.

At the third floor, the fireman said:

'Lucky it was no longer lived in.'

Ruth did not know how long he had been talking to her. She learned that, though the fire had been ferocious, they had managed to control it and it had not spread to any of the adjoining buildings, but that the whole street was being evacuated on account of the dangerous smoke.

'How did it happen?' asked Ruth, as they reached the ground floor.

'I just told you,' said the fireman, walking out onto the street and ushering her towards a large group of evacuees from her apartment block. He went to join his colleagues at the gates of the burning building.

Ruth was taken to the designated safety area a couple of blocks down the road. She was given a blanket and offered tea in a paper cup, which she refused. From here, she could still see the roof on fire. Looking up, there was the strange sensation of cold air and hot smoke against her face. Flashes of orange light tore up the night sky. On the roof of one of the adjoining buildings, a little above the worst of the smoke, a row of firemen stood like toy soldiers on top of a child's wardrobe.

Residents spilled out into the street from all directions: a dishevelled, sleep-soaked muddle. Shaking off slumber and shuffling to safety, blankets wrapped around their pyjamas, they were regrouping into tight family circles or wider bands of friends. Among them were a few faces Ruth recognised, but there was no one she knew. She had only been living in the flat for a couple of weeks, looking after it while her sister was away.

This was Ruth's first time living alone. Helen had gone travelling for three months just as Ruth was graduating and their parents suggested that Ruth take over the Brooklyn apartment and look for a job. It was a sensible move but Ruth had never been very good at making friends. It would have been one thing to move into a shared house but to move just like that – with no job and no sister – was something for which she had not been entirely prepared. And now this: she was standing alone among a crowd of anxious, exhausted people, with Helen's face still following her, a hangover from the dream.

Ruth looked about and saw the professor standing a careful distance from everyone else. Unlike Ruth, she appeared to be perfectly content being alone, her arms folded in front of her and her body angled away from the crowd to indicate that she did not wish to be approached. She wore a long tweed coat, and thick and clumsy-looking bed socks bunched over the sides of her heavy brown boots. Ruth watched as she drew a pack of cigarettes from one pocket and a bright metal lighter from another. As she lit up, her eyes met Ruth's, just for a moment, and she nodded. Ruth nodded back but turned away, not wishing to intrude on the professor's solitude.

Since Ruth moved in, they had met on the shared landing several times, never exchanging more than a few simple words, though Ruth had always tried to initiate a conversation. As much as she was nervous, even shy, in the company of her peers, Ruth enjoyed the company of old people. It had never been a chore to her to visit her grandparents, as it had been for her other siblings. Ruth loved to listen to them talk and to feel reassured by the solidity of their opinions. They knew what they liked. Others found this obstinate, but for Ruth it was a source of great comfort.

Ruth was offered another cup of tea, and this time she accepted. She drank half and let the rest go cold. Someone took the cup from her hands and replaced it with a fresh one. It was only when the fire had been reduced to smouldering ashes that they were allowed back to their end of the street and into their building.

When Ruth reached her sister's flat on the sixth floor, she found the professor lingering on the landing.

'Are you all right?' said Ruth. 'Do you have your key?'

'Yes,' said the professor, 'but I was wondering, would you come in for a drink? I thought you might be shaken up.'

'Thank you,' said Ruth, 'Yes,' and she followed the professor through the door.

The professor's flat was modestly decorated, the most elaborate item an ornate writing desk by the window. On it stood a large, pale-blue typewriter and a three-tiered letter-holder laden with envelopes and postcards. The professor indicated that Ruth should sit in one of two high-backed armchairs in the middle of the room. She walked over to the kitchen and returned with two large cut-glass tumblers, half filled with whisky. The smallest mouthful warmed her all the way through. The professor sat down in the other chair, holding her tumbler firmly with two hands. Ruth saw that her shoulders were trembling.

'Are you cold?' she said.

'A little,' said the professor. 'Perhaps you can fetch me a blanket from over there?' The professor pointed to a large chest on the far side of the room. Ruth put down her drink and went to get the blanket. She was surprised when the professor leant forwards to let Ruth drape it over her shoulders.

The professor said nothing so they sat in silence a while, sipping their drinks. Ruth was taking it slowly but the professor drank quickly and soon got up to pour herself a second. When she sat down again she was holding a book. She held it out towards Ruth.

'Would you read it to me?' she said.

'Of course,' said Ruth, and reached over to take the book from her hand.

Ruth looked at the book more closely: a slim

volume, barely a novella, with a pretty orange cover and gold lettering.

She began to read. After the first ten pages, the professor closed her eyes and fell asleep. For a while, Ruth was not sure whether she was really asleep, or just dozing, so she carried on until she was approximately halfway through.

Before leaving, Ruth took the second blanket and spread it over the professor, tucking it in gently behind her knees as she had done when her grandparents were very old. She let herself out, making sure that the latch was down. It was not until she was back in her own apartment that Ruth realised she had brought the book in with her.

Invigorated by the events of the night, Ruth found that she was not in the least inclined to sleep, so she sat in bed and read to the end of the book. It was a strange and winding tale, foreboding and ominous. Ruth felt sure that the story would end badly; so sure, in fact, that when she reached the last page she was surprised and heartened to find that everything turned out quite well. She could not explain why, but the fact that the book had such a pleasing ending only increased her fondness for the professor.

In the morning, she knocked on the professor's door but there was no answer. Ruth went back to her flat and made a cup of coffee. Half an hour later, she tried again, but there was still no reply. She decided she would slip a note under the door.

She took some nice paper and a black pen from Helen's desk and in the neatest handwriting she could manage – she had a sense that the professor would appreciate neatness – she wrote a note informing her that the little book was safe in her possession and that she would keep it until such a time as might be convenient for the professor to pick it up. She slipped the note under the door and went on with her day.

Weeks passed and the professor made no response. Ruth got into the habit of listening for the professor's footsteps on the landing, but she never managed to catch her going in or out. From time to time, Ruth would hear the shuffling of furniture or the clatter of crockery coming from the apartment across the landing. On these occasions, she would scuttle across and knock on the professor's door, but there was never any answer.

When Helen returned, Ruth told her about the fire and the professor and the book, but she could not quite describe the need she felt to see the professor once again, to return the book in person. As Ruth packed up her things, she placed the little orange book in her satchel several times, but each time she had taken it out again.

Carrying her luggage out onto the landing, Ruth kept hoping that the professor would be roused by the noise and open her door, but nothing happened. Ruth and Helen carried her belongings down to the taxi that was waiting outside. Helen stepped forward to give Ruth a hug, when Ruth said:

'I think I've forgotten something.'

Helen handed her the key and Ruth ran back inside. At the professor's door, Ruth stood and knocked for the very last time. She was sure that she heard footsteps inside but there was no answer, and Ruth was left to wonder what it was that she had done so very wrong.

Mirrorball

I am nine years old: a pathetic, sickly creature, always catching colds, infections, whatever's going round. Skinny and weak, I find myself submerged in delirious fever more often than not. My father takes more interest in me than is usual, possibly because I am there, in the flat, all of the time.

On one occasion, he wraps me up in an old winter jumper of his and takes me down to the club before opening. He shows me the decks and lets me play one of his records. He picks songs for me that he thinks I will like and, to my surprise, he is good at it. I watch carefully as he lifts the vinyl over the spike, taking note of the needle, the knobs, the speed settings and the filing of the cardboard cases. This goes on until I am too weak to stand up any longer and he takes me back to bed.

He tucks me in and declares that he is going to read me a story. I am instructed to try to stay awake for a little bit longer because first he has to find the book he wants to read. He is gone a long time. There is the swish of boxes and the clunk of suitcases in his bedroom, which is the room above mine. When he comes back, he has in his hands a small book with an ornate cover in green and blue. He sits near my head and opens the book at the first page. I see that the cover is printed with a photograph of a tapestry. It depicts an apricot tree with two birds perched on its twirling branches. It is not symmetrical but I like it very much. The birds, I deduce, must be woodpeckers, as the story is the story of Picus. My father reads to me with a voice that rings with genuine excitement. I languish in my fever, swirling the words around the bright fog in my head. When my father says goodnight, he puts the book on the floor beside me. Once he has left the room, I thrust out a goose-pimpled arm and bring it up under the covers.

I am ten years old and Lucrezia is taking me shopping. My father is in a terror of a mood and she will not leave me alone with him, even though she knows I am accustomed and that I learned long ago how to look after myself without him noticing me.

'You need a treat,' she says. 'When was the last time anyone took you shopping?'

No one has ever taken me shopping. My clothes are a medley of things that other women have left behind, my father's unwanted shirts and a pair of leggings I borrowed from someone at school after gym class and never returned.

It is a day of miracle cures, pocket-sized treasures, the sensuous pleasures of silk, velvet and suede; a day filled with a new vocabulary. There are *plackets, pleats, peplum*; *selvedges, gussets* and *epaulettes*; jackets in *brocade* and shimmering *jacquard*; dresses are *ruched, tucked* and *pinned*; silk is brushed and crushed. There are potions, too – potions that are normally locked away in a drawer of Lucrezia's dressing table. Lucrezia buys hair dye, face cream and perfume. I am allowed to carry the little black-and-white bag that holds the scent. She buys me a set of nail varnishes called Molten Metals. There are four colours: gold, silver, bronze and a luminous white shade called *Man in the Moon*. Lipsticks have names, too; Lucrezia wears *Rio Fanfare*, a vibrant red. She pronounces it the Italian way – Rio Fan*farr*ay. She won't, however, buy the shade of red she likes the best, because it's called Number Seven Red, and Lucrezia cannot stand the number seven. She says it's bad luck, though she will never tell me why.

At home, in my bedroom, while Lucrezia is unloading her purchases, I draw a picture of a large, red exotic flower, which I assume to be a Rio Fanfare.

At around half past ten, when I am still too excited about it all to be able to sleep, Lucrezia lets me come down with her to the club. Just for a few minutes, she says, so I can see the people coming in. My father is on the decks and he won't cause any trouble, even if he sees me.

'And in the morning?' I say.

'He won't remember,' says Lucrezia.

She is wearing a long, one-shoulder dress in pale grey and enormous chandelier earrings. We stand at the top of the spiral staircase that leads down to the dance floor, watching the club fill up from the basement door. They are smart, glamorous, glittering people, mostly wearing bright colours and some with brightly coloured hair. But there is also something messy about them. None have Lucrezia's grace.

There are so many mirrors on the walls of the club that wherever you look you seem to get a different version of the same view. One of my favourite things to do is to try to follow the spots of light reflected by the mirrorball that hangs from a long wire in the centre of the room. I can never manage it for very long. As soon as a spot hits a mirror, it merges with other spots and I get dizzy trying to separate one from the next.

'Will you go down and join them when I go to bed?' I say.

'Maybe for a while,' she says. 'A lot of the time I stand here, though.'

'Don't you dance?' I say.

'I only dance with my friends,' she says. 'And you.'

I turn to look at Lucrezia. I am so proud of her.

I am eleven years old, a couple of months into high school, and I am learning that nobody cares if I am not there. If I skip a class or two, or even a full day, most of the time I will not be missed. The truants at my school are thought to be battles-already-lost. Occasionally, someone gets expelled, but only if they drag one of the battles-still-being-fought-for into their midst. However, if we keep to ourselves, or, in my case, give all other students a wide berth, we are tolerated when we show our faces, as long as we behave. And even if I do get into trouble, I have my father's reputation to back me up.

I have been aware, for as long as I can remember, of the fame my father enjoys across the city. There is no end to the list of accusations levelled at him. Some are true, some are not. From time to time, the other kids at my school ask me questions about him, or pass on the gossip they overhear at the dinner table – 'my mum says your dad is a really bad man,' 'my mum says your dad has slept with all the whores in the Redwell Alley,' 'my dad says your dad once punched him in the gut.' I am never bullied; I am left alone. Even the teachers won't send letters back to my father. So I come and go as I please.

Lucrezia does not consider it her duty to see that I go to school. I ask her once why neither she nor my father punish me for bunking off, as other parents do.

'There are other ways to do things,' she says. 'I didn't spend much time in school.'

'What did you do?' I say.

'I just learned things a different way. I worked in my mother's café. I spent a lot of time watching people, I suppose.'

'Did you learn a lot that way?' I say.

'I learned to tell the people I admired from those I disliked,' Lucrezia says. 'Then I learned what it was that made the difference.'

'What made the difference?' I say.

'Style,' she says. 'Not money, style.'

❧

I am twelve years old. Lucrezia is away. Following her example, I am taking it upon myself to fill in the gaps of my education with only the things that please me. These are: drawing, dancing and biology. Still avoiding school, I become a member of the public library and borrow a book called *Beginning Ballet* and practise my *pliés*, *pas de chats* and *sautées* (*petites et grandes*) on the circular dance floor in the middle of the club, with my father's records providing the much-too-fast beats for my choreography. After a while, I give up with the ballet and dance around in the way that I've seen women dance in the club on Fridays and Saturdays, swaying my hips and making mermaid movements with my arms above my head.

Lucrezia phones at night, when she knows that my father will be down at the club. She asks me what I've been doing with my day and I answer truthfully. She asks me about the ballet book and I fetch it so that I can read to her the descriptions of the exercises.

'Perhaps we can do some ballet together when I get home,' she says.

I feel a great surge of relief when she says these words. She is definitely coming back.

❧

I am thirteen. I have a new best friend, whose name is George. We cut classes together, apart from art, which we deem to be of value. George has short curly hair which she wears messy, far messier than it would be if she were to leave it to its own devices. The carefully constructed disorder of her appearance is a source of pride. She dresses in plaid shirts several sizes too big, wearing them with leggings and walking boots. She does not walk so much as stomp.

We sit in the park by our school, feeding each other licorice laces that are a sickly neon red. She is the only person in school who has never been intimidated by me or the idea of my father.

Lucrezia and my father are fighting. They take turns at staying out all night, sharing the club between them. There are three, long nights over which they try to hash things out. On the first, they have loud and angry sex that even the music from the club below cannot disguise. On the second, my father slaps Lucrezia hard across the jawline and she creeps into my room with the red mark fresh. We do not speak but I hold her hand as I watch the mark begin to bleed dark colours into her cheek and down one side of her neck. That night, she shares my bed. We top and tail.

On the third night, they find a way through. They establish a language by which to communicate. The language they settle on is that of business and finance. They make plans for the club. Somehow, through these practical negotiations, their love revives.

I am fifteen. I am tall and – to everyone's surprise, not least my own – quite beautiful. Those who know Lucrezia see us walking down Apricot Grove arm in arm and stop to compliment her on her elegant daughter. Lucrezia is gracious and does not correct them. Men look at me. Lucrezia glares back.

I am sixteen years old and my father is turning the club into an art gallery. It will still be a club, of course, but it will also be an art gallery. The artist he has chosen to exhibit is called Xixi. We know he is serious when, for the very first time, he announces that he will not be opening the club as usual that Saturday night. Instead, he is setting it up for Xixi's private view. Lucrezia is livid.

Xixi is cold and, on occasion, downright rude. If it wasn't for her artwork I would scarcely have stopped to say hello. But there are her drawings, which I love.

Xixi works in charcoal and ink. The exhibition is a series of illustrations. They have titles like: 'A Lamb', 'A Wild Cat', 'A Pine Marten', 'A Badger Cub', 'An Adder'. While, on first glance, they might seem to be for children, they are rendered in such detail that they acquire a disturbing quality. Like a work of taxidermy, or a beautiful fur stole, there is a cruelty to their composition. My favourite is 'Roe Fawn'. The deer is positioned lying down, in the centre of the picture. Its neck and head are raised. Its tail bushes up a little at the end. Though at rest, it is clear that there is tension in the limbs. It is a creature ready to flee, waiting for a sign.

What I love most are the eyes: wide and bright, they are kind but also terribly afraid.

I go down to the club at night, just to look at it. I start to draw it myself. After just a few days, I have multiple copies by my own hand. I sleep late. There are dreams, the likes of which I have never before experienced. I lie motionless and over my body crawl paper cut-out fawns, grazing the surface of my skin with claws I can't quite feel. While other girls my age are dreaming of boys, I dream of lions, bears and swans, forcing me to the floor, threatening mysterious pleasures. When I wake, I am immediately alert, faintly sweating, with the same feverish glow I remember from my days of being sick as a child.

Xixi poses a problem to Lucrezia. After the private view is over, Xixi and my father stay down in the club, late into the night. The next morning, Lucrezia has words. She is quiet about this, and careful that Xixi does not see. To admit weakness in front of a competitor is not Lucrezia's style. I never learn precisely what is said. A careful threat is what I imagine. It proves effective. Within a day or two, Xixi is gone. The club reopens as a regular club. There is no more art. Xixi is not mentioned again. The dreams cease.

I am seventeen years old. It is late afternoon. My father is out. I have not seen him for several weeks. The last time he was home, he and Lucrezia were fighting, but not shouting like they did once, just talking in tired voices and sliding chairs around the kitchen floor as they stood up and sat down and stood up again. Lucrezia has reason to believe that he will be back soon, though I don't know how she has obtained this information. Before he arrives at the club, she wants to take me out for a drink.

'I want you to know what it's like to get drunk,' she says.

'I've had alcohol before,' I say.

'I know, but you've never been drunk.'

'I have, you know I have,' I say.

'No. You've been too drunk. You've been paralytic. It's not the same. You have to learn to be drunk.'

'OK,' I say. 'How do I do that?'

She talks to me for a while about the diverse effects of different kinds of drink. Wine makes you sleepy. Beer makes you full. Vodka makes you think you're not drunk until it's already too late. Gin can make you sad, but is otherwise an excellent choice. Cocktails should never be too sweet. Negronis and Martinis are smart. They also send the right message: class. Woo Woos, Mudslides and Long Island Ice Teas are bad news.

'Do we sell them at the club?' I ask.

'Of course we do. Everyone loves them,' she says.

She orders two Negronis. She tells me only to drink when she drinks. She orders some olives. We talk. I sip when she sips. I laugh when she laughs.

The next day, I go to see George. I take bottles of gin, Martini Rosso and Campari from the club's stock room. It is only five o'clock but completely dark and the air is thick with rush-hour fumes and the cigarettes of pedestrians. I have stowed the alcohol in a black leather drawstring bag that I wear nonchalantly over my shoulder. The weight of it makes it harder to walk in Lucrezia's high-heeled boots. When I get to George's, we sit by the electric heater in her room which she knows she is not supposed to use until it is December, but her mother is out with a man, which is causing George to communicate more angrily than usual. We mix our Negronis in tumblers and sit in companionable silence with the heat on our backs. George drinks her first glass in one gulp, slamming the tumbler down on the floor as she has seen angst-ridden people do on television programmes and in the movies. When the carpet absorbs the shock and there is no satisfying crack to complete the movement, she is disappointed.

'Shall I put on some music?' I say.

I find a record that I know from the club, one my

father likes to put on at the end of the night, while the staff wipe the tables and polish the glassware. I put an arm around her, half expecting her to shake me off, but instead she holds my hand and pulls it down to rest a fraction above her breasts. The warmth of her fuzzes in my palm.

I am eighteen years old when Lucrezia leaves in the night. There are small clues indicating her departure – missing hairbrushes in the bathroom, only almost-empty perfume bottles remaining – but nothing so clear as to enable me to see the truth of the situation. It is a couple of days before I run into my father, by which time I have already understood. We do not talk about it. Her name is not mentioned. He is no different and suffers no disruption to his usual routines. He does not drink or take drugs to greater or lesser excess. As such, I start to believe that he is immune to emotional responses. Perhaps Lucrezia lasted longer than the others, but, to him, she was still just one of many.

It soon becomes apparent that I am expected to take over from Lucrezia in terms of the club. I become a full-time bar manager. I do the ordering and the accounts. I write staff rotas and arrange private parties; I book DJs and live music acts. I stand at the top of the stairs looking down on the dance floor, wearing one of the three dresses that Lucrezia left behind.

My father begins to see me in a different light. I have his respect, and something else that I cannot place. He becomes more affectionate. One night, he kisses me on the neck while I am doing the washing up. Once, in the early hours of the morning, when I am coming to bed after a particularly busy night, he comes into my room with a glass of water and sits by my head, like he did, on occasion, when I was sick as a child.

I am nineteen years old when I tell him I no longer want to manage the club. He is furious. He pins me to the door. I grab the nearest thing – a frying pan – and hit his head with all the force I have. I knew, long before he did, what he would have gone on to do. While my father is reeling, I pack a bag. By the end of the week, I have moved in with George.

It takes me a long time to be able to talk about Lucrezia because, in her absence, I have become her. Not just in terms of the club. Away from my father, I am more like Lucrezia than ever before. In the evenings, George's mother makes macaroni cheese, fried chicken, sausages and mash, and I eat these dinners as though they are the haute cuisine Lucrezia brought back in boxes from her business suppers. I hold my cutlery as if it were light as air; I break up food into tiny morsels; I chew slowly; I never, ever clear my plate. Another thing: I have stolen her laugh. Nothing is genuinely funny to me anymore, so when I see it is required of me to laugh I throw back my head and let the mature sound of my cackle shake through my shoulders. I pin up my hair and wear dark-coloured lipstick. There are blisters on my feet from wearing her shoes. The only major difference is that Lucrezia liked to wear colour. Coloured skirts, print shirts, bright makeup, coloured tights, clashing shoes. She was always expertly put together – nobody could mix prints and palettes like she could. In contrast, I dress only in black. In part, this is because it was mostly black clothing that she left behind, but there is also something about black that makes me feel safe, like I can't go wrong.

I am twenty. I get a job at a PR firm called 'Pure'. After a few months, I move out of George's mother's place and into an apartment that I share with the new intern, which is paid for, largely, by her financial-adviser father.

When I see George, we air kiss and drink cocktails in cafés. That is: she drinks cocktails; I have moved a step ahead and drink vodka, neat, over ice. We are going through a phase of pretending not to be particularly interested in each others' lives. We are nonchalant about everything, especially the future. We do not know, at this point, the dangers of this. Eventually we will claw back some enthusiasm for our own lives but the enthusiasm we once shared for each other will be much harder to recover.

I am too busy being nonchalant to tell George how much I wish I could know if Lucrezia had ever tried to call me. Now that I am no longer living with my father, there is no way for her to reach me. But perhaps that's for the best. She didn't leave a note, after all. I find peace by telling myself that Lucrezia was smart and that she would have had her reasons.

I see Lucrezia again only once before I leave Edinburgh for good. She is coming out of the revolving doors at the bottom of 36 St Andrew's Square – one of the large financial buildings in close proximity to the PR firm. A cab pulls up right away and she clambers in. I have just enough time to make an inventory of her accoutrements: large diamond earrings, long fur coat, tweed trousers, red heels. As she opens the cab door I think I see a wedding ring on her hand, but there is not sufficient time to know for sure whether it is the right finger or the right kind of ring. Lucrezia does not look up. She does not see me.

I leave Pure when someone asks me to be a model in an advert for perfume: I am tall and slightly strange-looking in the way that, for a time, is deemed desirable. My eyes sit too far apart. From Lucrezia, I have inherited the art of inciting a sense of aspiration in others. Everyone wants to know where I am from. Such olive skin, such fair hair. I tell them I am half-Portuguese and this seems to be sufficient explanation. Modelling takes me to London, as I had hoped.

꙳

I am twenty-two years old, living in Soho, and there is a knock at the door. It is my father. He has come without warning. Without knowing what might be the right or the wrong thing to do, without even knowing what it is that I want to do, I invite him in.

'What are you doing here?' I say. 'You might have called.'

'I didn't know if you'd want to see me,' he says.

'Do you want to see me?' I say.

He says: 'I thought I should come.'

I can see in his face that he knows how pathetic this sounds. He is ashamed, but not of the past. And I am ashamed on his behalf. The shame is cancelling out his charisma, which was all he had left to redeem him. What he cannot realise is that his charm – that brilliant facade – is, in fact, the only excuse that I have for him. In the end, the performance is the one palatable thing he has to offer. Yet here he is trying to be genuine.

I ask all the questions.

I learn that he has moved to Glasgow, where he lives with a new wife, twenty years his junior, and her two young children. He runs a shop selling second-hand records. The teenagers love it, he says.

When I feel that we have exchanged sufficient information, I ask him the one thing of importance.

'Have you seen Lucrezia?' I say.

He looks surprised. It has never occurred to him that for me Lucrezia was not a temporary fixture; that while the two of them were only playing at family life, they were my family.

'No,' he says. 'I've no idea where she is.'

When he leaves, I tell him not to come back. He nods. I think he is relieved.

❧

The next morning, I am called in for a shoot at a disused warehouse with a large spiral staircase. The photographer stands at the bottom of the stairs while I am at the top. I am instructed to walk down the stairs as slowly as I can without wobbling. I have been told to 'think regal and ethereal'. I think: Lucrezia. I remember, with precision, the way she held her arms, the exact positioning of her neck, the movement in her hips as she walked. It all comes together. It was not for nothing, I think, and I am so happy in that moment. I spend the rest of the afternoon sitting in a café. I pretend to be reading magazines but really I am watching, deciding whom I do and don't like and what it is that makes the difference.

Rock Sparrow

When it is time for us to go, I step towards my father but he pushes me away. He reaches into his pocket and finds a packet of cigarettes which he hands to my brother, Adi. He turns to me and shakes my hand. It is as if he is saying goodbye to an old business partner, at the end of some complex nego- tiation, rather than a son. I tell him I will write to him. He nods. We turn and leave.

As we walk, Adi kicks stones on the ground, sometimes sending them flying in high arcs. I know he is angry. He thinks our father should be encouraging us or applauding us for our bravery; either that, or begging us to stay. It's the nonchalance, the apathy, he finds offensive. But this is how it is.

The pick-up point is a factory car park behind the water tower. It is a fifteen-minute walk. Adi smokes cigarette after cigarette and is quiet. We arrive early. There is a man standing in front of an open-back truck. He has thick stubble and I notice his jeans are ripped. The sleeves of his shirt are rolled up past his elbows.

We approach. The man looks at Adi's cigarette.

'You got a spare one of those?' he says.

Adi hands him the box.

We stand, kicking the dust into clouds until the man gets into the driver's seat.

'It's time to go,' he says.

We climb in the back.

It is then that I notice a young boy sitting in the front. He is introduced to us as Paul. He is the driver's cousin. The driver's name is Cam. Apart from that, and his liking for cheap cigarettes, I know nothing about him.

The first part of the journey goes quickly. The highway is empty and we drive at speed. In the back of the truck, I watch the ants make patterns in the dust on the floor. Adi, always more at ease, chats to the others. He flits from subject to subject, relating anecdotes I know well. As he talks, the city behind us disappears into the horizon.

We have lived there all our lives. Our childhood was written in its helter-skelter streets, in the spaces under walnut trees where we sat with our friends after school, playing checkers and noughts and crosses with twigs, empty nutshells and stones.

Our house sat between the bird market and the alley of straw sellers. Every once in a while, a bird would escape from a cage and swoop in through the kitchen door. The stall holder would rush in after it, screaming obscenities as it darted about the room. My father, disturbed by the commotion, would appear in the doorway and command silence. He would raise one hand and wait for the bird to flutter over. He would hold the bird on his forefinger and look at it carefully.

'Do you know this one?' he would say to me.

I always shook my head, whether I knew the bird or not, and my father would tell me its name, how it could be identified by its markings. He made strange noises in the back of his throat in imitation of its song.

After a couple of hours in the truck, we stop for lunch at a roadside shack. We have kofta kebabs and cola. The meat is slick with oil. We mop it up with dry bread from a basket. When we have finished, we go outside to smoke.

Paul points at my cigarette.

'You know it's bad for you,' he says.

I turn to face the boy. He is small. To look at him, he might be six, possibly seven years old, but from the way he talks I think he must be older. He has a muddle of thick curly hair. He holds a book beneath one arm.

'What are you reading?' I ask. Paul holds up the cover. *Intermediate English*.

'Intermediate, eh?' I say. Paul grins.

We return to the truck. Adi gets in the front seat with Cam and Paul sits in the back with me. I take the book and test Paul on the words he has already learnt. He is good. He remembers everything and, at the end of the test, he smiles broadly.

We reach the border at dusk. There is a long wait. Cam gets out and goes to speak to the guards. He hands over an envelope full of cash and several cartons of cigars. They seem to have a lot of questions. They point at the truck and make notes. One of them tears a sheet of paper from a notebook and hands it to Cam.

128

Cam turns and walks back to the truck. We watch him but he does not look at us. His hands are in his pockets, his shoulders high up around his ears.

There is a government official doing checks, he says. We can't cross tonight, we will have to wait forty-eight hours. He has been given directions to a small hotel an hour's drive away.

He pulls the piece of paper from his pocket. A list of directions.

'You gave them the cigars?' says Paul.

'Yes, I gave them the cigars,' says Cam. He lights a cigarette.

I look over at Adi. He is stamping one foot on the ground, over and over. He is angry. 'I bet you're in on this, aren't you?' he says to Cam. 'I've heard about scams like this. You're taking us to some dump owned by your family, stretching your profits.'

I want to do something but I know there is nothing I can say.

Cam looks at Adi. He shrugs before climbing back into the driver's seat. I get in the back with Paul, hoping Adi will follow. Adi stays where he is. His gaze is fixed on the wire fence at the edge of our country. Birds are perched, preening themselves between the barbs.

Adi bends down and picks up a rock. It is large

and jagged, about the size of his fist. For a moment I think he will throw it at Cam.

'Adi,' I say.

I begin to get down from the truck but Adi runs towards the border. He hurls the rock over the metal gate and the birds scatter. Guards on either side raise their guns. Adi stands his ground. His shoulders are shaking. I do not know if he is angry or scared. One step further, I think, and they will shoot. At Adi and at us. There is nowhere to hide.

Adi holds up his hands, in a gesture of compliance. He walks, still facing the guards, back towards us. After twenty paces the guards lower their arms and Adi turns around. He runs the rest of the way to the truck. He gets in the back, sits down but does not speak. His eyes fix on the space between his feet. I sit down too. Cam starts the engine and everybody jumps.

Once we are back on the road, Cam says: 'Don't you ever pull a stunt like that again.'

Adi says nothing.

'You hear me?' says Cam.

Adi nods.

'You put us in danger, you can get out and walk,' says Cam.

Still, Adi is silent.

'Understood?' says Cam.

'Yes, sir,' says Adi, in the way he used to speak to our father after a telling off.

The hotel is run down. Its pale blue exterior is crumbling away. The rooms are clean enough, but small. Each one has two narrow beds and a sink with a bar of dirty soap between the taps. The proprietress is thin and looks tired. There are streaks of grey through her hair.

'I cook in the morning,' she says. 'Whatever I make will last the day. If you want it hot and fresh, get your fill at breakfast.'

We nod.

'Thank you,' says Paul.

I put a hand on Adi's back. He moves away.

I look at Paul. He smiles at me. He has one hand in his satchel. He pulls out a brown-paper package. Inside, there are homemade biscuits.

'Want one?' he says. 'They're good.' I take one. They are good. Crumbs fall into my palm and I lick them off.

The day our mother died, there were biscuits she had made on the cooling rack in the kitchen. It was my first week at university. I was eighteen years old. Adi was not quite fourteen. The sky was overcast. The air was hot. There was no breeze. My father found her in the bedroom. She had hanged herself from an old beam using a belt of his for rope. Her sisters bathed the body, that night. They wrapped it up in white linen. Their whisperings to one another, their attention to their task, made Adi and me feel like intruders in our own home.

The funeral took place the next morning. The wake was small. For three days afterwards, the house was crowded with visitors, relatives and friends. Then everything was quiet.

My father took a job in an office. He worked late. He was rarely home before midnight. When he came home, he sat in the yard outside and smoked. The kitchen got dirty, and even the birds sensed the change. When they escaped they simply blundered around the market then vanished into the horizon.

The invasion came a few months later. Foreign military took over the streets. A temporary government was created. Protests followed. The sound of the birds was replaced with distant gunfire and occasional explosions. Most of the attacks were in the centre of town but there were times when they came closer and the house shook. The mosque at the end

of our street was bombed. A few days later, the
market closed down. There was no business, no trade,
and my father lost his job. He came home.

He made a bedroom downstairs, piled high with
books of all kinds. He put a mattress on the floor and
washed himself in the utility kitchen. He avoided all
other parts of the house. When he ate, he ate alone.
He snacked on things he found: a triangle of bread,
a satsuma or a handful of seeds. I helped Adi with
his homework. I made sure he came home at a reason-
able hour. I cooked for us, following the recipes my
mother had jotted down in notebooks or cut from
magazines. When he was angry, it was always me who
calmed him down. And then we left.

We stay two nights in the hotel. On the morning of
the third day, we are ready to leave. Paul is missing.
Adi and Cam wait by the truck. I search.

At the back of the hotel there is a courtyard. I
look around. It is bare but for a couple of wooden
planks, three gas canisters and an empty chicken
coop. Paul is crouched on the ground in the far
corner. In front of him is his book. He has a pen in
his hand. At the top of the page is a small dark
shape.

'What are you doing down there?' I say.

'Drawing,' he replies.

'Drawing what?'

'Come and look.'

I walk over to Paul. Above the book is a small dead bird. It is a dirty beige-coloured thing. It has a thin black line down the centre of its head and small black marks on its feathers.

I pick up one of Paul's pencils and poke the bird's wing.

'Do you know what it is?' I say.

'No,' he says.

'It's a rock sparrow,' I say. 'They sing very loudly.'

'Not this one,' says Paul.

'No,' I say. 'Not this one.'

'How does it sound?'

I make a high-pitched noise and Paul laughs. He throws back his head and slaps his palms on his knees.

I move closer to get a better look at the picture he has drawn.

'You're very good,' I say.

He has traced the outline of the body, the shape of the beak, one round eye and half a wing. He has drawn over the top of a vocabulary list: *(in) the mountains, (at) the beach, (in) the city.*

'I haven't coloured it in,' he says, 'so I can still see the words.'

I nod.

'Should we do something with it?' Paul says, pointing at the bird.

'No,' I say. 'It's time to go. The others are waiting.'

Paul does not move. He looks at the bird and then at me.

In a dry patch of earth at one end of the yard, we dig a small hole with our hands. I pick up the bird and place it gently in the ground. Paul sits with his head bowed as I cover its body with earth and level the top. We leave.

At the border, the guards let us pass. Once we have crossed over, I write a letter to my father. My pen jolts with every bump in the road. I describe the sparrow and its markings. I tell him about Paul and the way he had laughed when I made the noise. I tell him about the birds on the wire at the border crossing, preening themselves in the sun. I do not tell him about the rock Adi threw. I do not mention the hotel. I say nothing of the journey ahead.

Still

PART ONE

Every year, when the plum tree had lost its leaves, my father would take a photograph. From the moment the air turned cool, we would keep a close eye on it, watching the shades of green become gold, waiting for the last leaf to drop.

Some years we would wake to find the tree suddenly bare, the remaining few leaves having fallen in the night. At other times, the last leaves would struggle on through the morning but, later in the day, they would be gone. Then there were the handful of more memorable occasions when, on looking out of the

139

window – that of his bedroom or the dining room below – either my father or I or both of us together would catch the last leaf as it came fluttering down to the ground, watching it curl and flip through the air, before resting weightless on the grass or skipping away on the cusp of a breeze.

'It's time, son,' he would say, and fetch his camera.

At that time of year it was not quite winter-cold, but the seasons were shifting. Fewer clouds gathered overhead. The daylight sharpened and the materials of the garden – the stone path, the greenhouse, the antique table, the ironwork chairs and the plum tree itself – appeared in greater definition. The residual warmth of summer evaporated.

A dip in the land meant the scattered houses beyond remained invisible. In this way, the photographs made it appear as though the tree were the only marker on the horizon for miles around.

I would stand by his side and wait for the click, followed by the familiar winding of the film. He only ever took one shot. If the weather was bad, my father would make me watch through the dining-room window. I would kneel on the deep wooden sill, looking at him through the central pane. At this distance, my mind became active. It was my mother's tree, a memorial planted shortly after she died; I was four months old.

My father developed the photographs himself in the basement. The images were large – ten by twelve inches, black and white. He mounted them on pieces of black sugar-paper cut to size to give a narrow frame. When he had finished, he would come to show me his work and I would nod my approval, commenting on the particulars: the position of the clouds, the blur of a breeze, the quality of the light. Each one was dated, numbered and stored in a heavy wooden box that he kept in the cupboard under the stairs.

I was often alone. Sometimes, if I was bored, I would take the pictures out, arranging them in patterns on the carpet or sorting them into piles. The few friends I had lived in the next village and, while on summer days I was glad to make the journey on my bike, when autumn closed in my father became anxious and I chose not to anguish him further by straying out of doors. In any case, I liked to be there, in the house, reordering the pictures, always looking for the most pleasing arrangement.

It would be easy to imagine that the photographs are all alike. The plum tree did not grow a great deal over the years and, as far as was possible, its shape was maintained by frequent pruning. Even so, while certain of the photographs bore close resemblance to one another, others differed so wildly that, had the backdrop not been so consistent – had the fields been dug up for housing, say, or the farmer chosen to plant a new crop – it would be easy to say that these were different plum trees from different lands. A certain kind of evening light made one image pale and over-bright, the sun burning a hole in part of the trunk. In another, the wind had torn through the upper branches and made them blur. In a third, the tree was ink-black against a perfect sky so that it almost looked like a drawing.

There are a number of ways to categorise the photographs. From the position of the sun and the quality of the light, it is possible to identify those taken in the morning, the afternoon and at sunset. Some skies were dull, some were clear with an occasional cloud, and others stretched away smoothly, disturbed only by the grain of the lens. But when I was in my teens I preferred the simplest method: to make two piles, one for before and one for after the storm.

In the winter between the tenth and the eleventh photographs, there was a night of crazed winds, lashing rain and forked lightning. Disturbed by the commotion, I ran into my father's room and we lay in bed holding onto one another. We didn't think of the tree until the morning. The largest branch on the right side of the tree, and others leading off from it, had split and fallen. We stood at the dining-room window, looking out at the felled branch lying broken on the lawn. In the pictures that followed you could chart small changes in the tree; the branches on the left sunk lower as it began to lean, falling – too slowly to see – towards the earth.

There were other exceptions. Of the thirty-two pictures he took, only one – the eighteenth – was in colour.

'Why, when the rest are black and white?' I had said. I looked forward to the developed picture and this move away from tradition set me on edge.

'Because when I took it the sky was so grey,' he said.

Alone, the picture could pose as monochrome. It was only when it was placed among the others that its particular subtlety and warmth of tone became evident. My father held it against the photograph from the previous year.

'It was a stupid thing to do,' he said. 'I made a mistake.'

Shortly after my eighteenth birthday, I enrolled to study architectural design at the University of Valencia,

leaving my father alone in the house. He had encour-
aged me, then resigned himself to the change. I arrived
in the summer, a month or two before term began,
and, at the time, I had little thought for autumn. When
the days of September ran out and the heat endured,
an uneasiness crept in. Every few days, I would phone
home and enquire about the tree.

'A few more have gone,' he would say. 'One or two
fallen, I think. Though it's early yet.'

In Valencia, autumn was never cool. When it finally
arrived, the air was only a little altered and the light
the same. Trees were slow to lose their leaves and
many never did. Instead, the habit of Valencian leaves
was to grow limp and hang, undead, waiting for a
cold that would not come.

One November afternoon, I called him and he
said: 'They've all gone. I took the picture.'

When I went home for the winter holidays that
year we did not talk about the photograph I'd missed,
the first in almost twenty years.

During my third year abroad, I decided to go home
for the photograph. I called a few weeks ahead and
had a long conversation with my father regarding the
precise timing of my trip and over which days I would
have the best chance of catching the plum tree as it
lost its last leaves. He kept careful records of his work

and, looking at the dates of the photographs, he concluded that the most opportune window was between the fourteenth and the twenty-second of November. I made my arrangements accordingly.

When I arrived back it was the fourteenth. Eight leaves remained on the tree. The next day there were six, then five. On the fourth, fifth and sixth days there were three. After a week had gone by, only two leaves remained and on 22 November – the day of my departure – there was one leaf left. I had packed my bags the night before and my train to the airport was at half past one. We would need to leave the house at twelve. By the time we finished breakfast it was nine.

'Still one, still one,' my father said, looking out of the dining room window. Then, when the last of the coffee had been drunk, he said: 'I know what to do.'

'You can't take the picture with the leaf still there,' I said.

'Of course not,' said my father.

I followed him out the back door. Instead of assuming his usual position on the path, he kept on walking towards the tree. He reached up and before I could stop him he had the last leaf in his hand. It was stubborn and it took a hard tug to free it from its branch. He stuffed the leaf into the back pocket of his jeans and moved away from the tree, the camera slung around his neck. He took the picture, the twenty-first in the sequence. The ritual was broken, the archive contaminated. He had ignored his own rules. I felt ashamed that he had done this for my sake, because I no longer lived there, because we were both getting older, and who knew how many photographs were left?

PART TWO

When I graduated from Valencia, I got an apprenticeship in New York. My father was thrilled, and for the first time since I had left home, I sensed that we had come to some kind of understanding. I no longer asked about the tree; he never mentioned it. For many years, I did not go home. Things were happening for me in New York, which was at once a truth and an apology.

After a year in the city, I met Laura. An American and a dancer, lively, always laughing, with a large and close-knit family upstate: a heritage utterly removed from the almost silent world of my childhood. We went to art galleries. She took me to the opera. I showed her my projects and she brought me along to rehearsal. When she walked, there was a slight turn-out in her feet.

The spring before the very last picture was taken, Laura and I got engaged. That same April, I took her home to meet my father. The plum tree was in full bloom. We sat beneath it, drinking prosecco and laughing like children. Laura charmed him. She seemed to have an effect on his character: he became playful, gracious, even stylish. He took great pride in the way he served us dinner and in the mornings he laid on lavish breakfasts, with pastries, fruits, breads and jams the likes of which I had never known him buy before. We stayed a full week, during which time neither my father nor I made any mention of the catalogue of photographs under the stairs. I remember having wanted to ask him if he continued to honour the tradition, but something – whether a sense of embarrassment or ritualistic sanctity, I don't know – prevented me.

He died the following winter. An aneurism, aged sixty-two. It was quick and without pain, they said. I went alone to make the arrangements for the funeral. I called the vicar and asked him to make an announcement. The local newspaper was informed. When the day of the funeral came, the church was packed; pews crammed, people standing at the back. Even more turned up for the wake at the Drifter's Inn on the other side of the village.

I had no idea he had so many friends. When I was a boy he had very few visitors. In fact, he had never exhibited much need of other company at all. But it seemed that once I left he became an active member of the community. He mowed the lawn of the cemetery and volunteered at the local school. He had even led a photography workshop at the village hall.

Laura, who had come for the funeral, went back to New York while I stayed on for a few more weeks. There was no good reason to hold on to the house. I called an estate agent and it was sold within two months. A few bits of furniture, pieces of my mother's jewellery he had kept, and other items I had loved or that seemed important somehow, were shipped to New York; among them, of course, were the photographs.

They remained in their box on a low shelf in my study for many years. Whenever I looked at the box, I told myself I was keeping them there for their protection, so they would not fade. In the end, it was Laura who unearthed them. She was pregnant at the time and, unable to dance, had set her mind on clearing out the house. It was more than a decade since he had died.

I was in the kitchen when she came to find me:

'Did you take these?' she said, holding up an image in each hand. 'Where did you find a tree like that in New York?'

She was oddly suspicious, as though I might have been sneaking out to take pictures of trees behind her back.

'You know that tree,' I said. 'You've seen it. It's the plum tree in my father's garden.'

She looked blank.

'You sat beneath it once to toast our engagement,' I said.

'But it looks so different,' said Laura, looking at one of the pictures from before the storm.

'I know, but that's the one.'

'Did you take them?' she said.

'No, he did.'

'Well,' she said, calmer, 'they're lovely. You should do something with them. Put them up.'

'In the house?'

'If you like, or in your office, or in a gallery somewhere.'

I laughed. 'Let me think,' I said.

At that time I was working for a firm on the Upper

West Side. I made models of the cities of the future, the ones that my child would come to know. On the ground floor of the building was a printing office, run by a woman called Lin. She was softly spoken, almost to the point of being inaudible, as though the incessant back-and-forth noise of the printers and copiers had quietened her over the years.

'I need a favour,' I said. I showed her the pictures. She looked at them with curiosity but made no comment. I asked for ten copies of each. She raised an eyebrow.

'Is that too much?' I asked.

She shook her head. 'Come back in three days.'

When I went back, she handed me the images, all three hundred and twenty of them, plus the thirty-two originals, in a cardboard box. I reached for my wallet and took out a few notes.

'No need,' she said.

'Are you sure?'

'I made an extra copy of this one,' she said. It was the one in colour. 'I'm going to put it in my kitchen,' she said. 'It looks like a tree from my grandfather's garden.'

'In Japan?'

'I know,' she said, 'but it does.'

'And the others?'

'I know, they're all the same. But this one looks more like the one I remember than the rest.'

I set to work. On the back of each print I placed a sticker with the date of capture and numbered them in sequence. I hung one set of copies across three walls of my study at home. I knew that the light in the room was uneven and that some of the pictures would fade faster than others. But now that there were so many copies, it was hard to imagine a time when they would all be faded. They would outlive me, at least. When all the pictures were arranged, I stood before them, looking carefully. When I stopped at one, perhaps the fourth or the fifth, a warmth crept over my shoulders, radiating from the memory of the way my father's back almost touched the dining-room window. I felt the stone path beneath my feet and the change of air against my cheeks. Though I had never taken a single photograph in that house, I felt the weight and the coolness of the camera in my hands and the presence of a young boy at my side, watching and waiting for the click of the big black button, the winding of the film, the tap on the shoulder that meant it was time to go back inside.

Laura gave birth to a girl, a long-limbed little thing with a shock of fair hair. We named her Carla, after

Carla Fracci. She couldn't take her eyes off us, whether we were working or cooking or sitting down at the end of the day to listen to music. It was as if she were watching over us, and not the other way round. When she was very small, I used to carry her into my study. I held her to my chest so that her head poked over my shoulder. I walked her slowly from one photograph to the next, moving with my back to the frames, so that Carla could get the best view. I pictured each image as she arrived at it, her breathing soft and steady in my ear.

When she was old enough I gave her a set of copies. Just as I had done, she liked to reorder and reorganise the images, dividing them up, placing them in grids or columns or zigzags across the floor.

At school, her subject was art and she came home, night after night, with some new painting or drawing rolled up under her arm. At sixteen, she went to art school. At eighteen she decided to go professional, living at home, saving money for her first show. She was friends with the right people. She had Laura's quiet confidence. I never doubted she would succeed. We gave her the dining room to use as a studio, taking our meals at the kitchen table. For two whole years she wouldn't show us a thing.

In that time, I learned that the old house was no

longer there. The family who had bought it sold it on to developers, who had simply waited for the right time to build. They razed it to the ground and, presumably, the plum tree with it. I was suddenly aware that there were no photographs of anything else. My father had not documented my childhood the way most parents do, the way we had with Carla. There were no pictures of our Christmases, our outings to the city, my football matches or school plays, though he had attended them all. There was only the plum tree; thirty-two versions of it, and all more or less the same. Soon after, I took the photographs down and replaced them with bits of Carla's work. I left them in their frames and piled them into a box.

When Carla was twenty, and I was as old as my father had been when he died, she unveiled the project. It could not be done at home, she said, so she hired a cheap space in Brooklyn, a fifteen-foot square room with no windows and painted white. When she ushered us in, it was pitch black. She held some manner of remote control in her hand. She clicked a button and the room filled with light, which cast peculiar shadows on the wall.

The back wall was filled with miniature spotlights and each light was fitted with a lens from which the shadows were generated. As my eyes adjusted, I began to recognise the shapes on the wall as images of the plum tree. I counted the lights. Thirty-two lenses for thirty-two photographs. I looked more closely at the projections, identifying the tree before the storm and after it, the pictures with clear skies, with dark skies, with clouds. The shadows were all different sizes, the images magnified to different degrees and tilted to fall upon different parts of the room. In the middle of one wall, something strange caught my eye. I walked towards it. The tone of the shadow was faintly blue, and the sky not quite clean.

'The one in colour,' I said.

Carla nodded.

She handed me the remote control. There were thirty-two buttons.

'How did you do this?' I said.

'Magic.'

'How long can we stay?'

'As long as you like.'

I took them on a tour of the room. I told them about the storm, the years I had missed, the years I returned. We clicked the lights on and off, all three of us, and adjusted the angles, moving the images from ceiling to walls to floor, in order to find the most pleasing arrangement.

Blind Water Pass

Lily stoops to pull a plastic bottle from the lower branches of a mountain bush. The bottle cracks and buckles as she squeezes out the air. She throws it over her shoulder to land in the large wicker basket strapped to her back. Ing, Granny Bud's old goat, is following her down the path, nuzzling at her ankles. Lily tries to nudge her away but Ing persists, so she turns and with both hands pushes the old goat back up the slope towards the house.

Lily is the youngest of the bottle collectors on Blind Water Pass, but she only does it in the holidays. The rest of the year, she lives in the city, spending school nights in one of the long girls' dormitories and the weekends at her parents' apartment on the outskirts of the Chemical Industry Park. But throughout the summer Lily stays with Granny Bud. Recycling earns her a small amount of money, which she keeps for herself. She can make far more from tips and this she gives to Granny Bud, though Granny Bud presumes it to be the other way around.

Blind Water Pass is quiet today, with fewer tourists than is usual in high summer. Wet weather has made the trail more dangerous, with sections of the path becoming quagmire and rocks overhead loosening under the weight of falling rain. For the first part of the week, the path was closed, but it has since reopened. Warning signs were placed at the foot of the gorge: perhaps somebody has forgotten to take them down. Or perhaps the tourists are starting late, and have yet to climb as high as Lily's grandmother's house.

The day is hot and luminous and the mud is drying fast. Even the water moving below seems gentler. On days like today, when the sky is bright blue light, the view still has the power to make Lily look up from her work and take a few slow breaths of gratitude.

Blind Water Pass runs ten miles along a ridge above the Silver River and has a guidebook reputation for

being more than a long walk: over the years it has
become a spiritual undertaking. Though the mountain spirits have always had a role to play in the daily
lives of the residents, the path itself has no particular
significance beyond its historical interest. But for the
tourists, it has become a meditative journey, a way
to still the passions of the mind.

At one time, the pass had two routes: the high
road, which remains, and the low road, scraping
closer to water level, which no one has used for
several years. It used to be that the low road was
the easier path to take, before they built the dam.
Where there were once glassy planes and calm
corners for swimming, there are now swirling
torrents reaching high up the walls of the cliffs. For
a time, the locals fought to keep the low road open.
But after the twelfth drowning, it was closed for
good.

The remaining high road can be traversed in a
number of ways. Some visitors choose to make the
journey with the aid of a donkey and a guide. The
donkey carries them the first nine miles of the way –
almost as far as Granny Bud's house – before setting
them down to walk the final stretch, where the views
are the most spectacular and the trail quite flat.
However, most tourists will abandon their donkeys at

the waterfall, where a stream forms a thick water-sheet over the wide flat stones of the path. They don't trust their mountain donkeys to keep steady across this new challenge in the terrain, though the donkeys are more sure-footed than any tourist Lily has seen.

If they don't go by donkey, they walk, guiding themselves with a book, or as part of a tour, where a friendly local narrates the factual and mythical histories of the trail along the way.

The Rock of Eternal Natality has been – for many, many centuries – a place for people to worship the gods and goddesses of fertility, either for the sake of biological reproduction, or for improved creativity, the fertility of the imagination and the mind.

In the early part of the fifth century, this was a trade route for tea. In more recent times of war, the recesses along the disappeared low road were used as hideouts for criminals. Now we use the trail not just to get a glimpse of the past, but to be closer to nature and to marvel at the majestic beauty of the mountains, to gasp at the force of the river below. [Everyone gasps.]

And here we come to the highest and most haunted place along the pass: Unfinished Hopelessness Cliff. Please take a moment to enjoy the view.

Once the tourists have completed their spiritual journey, they take the bus back into town. The road cuts through the cliffs in a network of tunnels and arrives at a small municipality comprised of a cluster of hostels, a couple of noodle bars and the train station. Next year, Blind Water Pass will be closed for ten months to make way for construction. The government are building what is already being hailed as the world's most elaborate funicular train, which will run the full length of the pass. Then there will be two kinds of tourists: those making spiritual pilgrimages and those riding the funicular to appreciate the spectacular vistas without physical exertion.

Usually, the only people walking down the pass, against the traffic of tourists, are people like Lily, with work to do. Some sell bottles of water kept in cool-boxes, others a range of international crackers: Japanese seaweed, sesame bites, cheese crisps and saltines. There are also souvenirs – the usual assortment, much the same as the ones they sell at the People's History Museum, not far from Lily's parents' house. Those who don't sell things, provide services. There are recyclers, like Lily, or holistic therapists offering weary travellers a quick massage or a herbal tea. Then there are the educators, people giving tours of the many micro-ecosystems to which Blind Water Pass plays host, or giving mini-lectures on spots of particular mythological significance. A few of the mountain workers are also residents, running the three cafés, and, around the half way mark, a B&B. The only other people who live there are very old, like Granny Bud: those who have never known anything beyond the ridges of the gorge.

As a girl, Granny Bud was a mountain farmhand, helping her parents make a living from the vege-tables and the herbs that grew in abundance towards the top of the pass. When she got older and had children of her own, the crops began to fail, leaving her without trade. So she started a new venture as a spirit guide, curing the people and working animals of their malevolent spirits and demons. With the power of her herbal remedies and incanta-tions, she even managed to bring life back into a few patches of mountain earth so that some of the farmers were able to revive a little of their old trade. When the tourists came, her role as local spirit guide shifted. To foreign visitors, she doled out herbal teas and home-made tonics and, later, read fortunes and palms. Yet whenever anxiety ran high among the locals, she was still the first to be called. Even now, every night when she comes home, Lily finds Granny Bud in the garden at the back of the house, with her arms outstretched and hands poised, scanning and assessing the disturbances of the spirit world.

The spirits have been restless for while. They are unhappy; the causes of their discontent accumulate and they no longer feel at home. First there was the arrival of the tourists, and then the building of the dam. With the construction of the funicular about to begin, their agitations have escalated. Granny Bud tries hard to still their nerves, to reassure them that the original residents of the pass still respect the old ways, but the spirits have become harder and harder to reach.

Lily meets her first tourists at the waterfall. A couple, standing on the far side, are consulting their guidebook, looking for instruction on how to cross. With their heads bent towards their book, Lily can get a good look at them without their noticing. They are both tall. The man has thick blond hair that curves around his chin into a scraggly beard. His nose is large and slightly red from the sun. The woman has finer features, a narrow nose and sharp cheekbones. Her skin is very pale and there are dark shadows beneath her eyes. The woman pulls her light-brown hair into a high ponytail that accentuates the angles of her face. Lily gives the bushes on her side of the waterfall a quick scan for discarded bottles, but Blind Water Pass has been so quiet of late she finds none. She coughs quietly, but with just enough noise to get the couple's attention, and, when they look up, she skips cleanly across the slick, wet stones in four light steps, getting as close to the cliff-edge as she can, knowing they will admire her grace and daring.

'Hello,' says the man, amused.

Lily gives a small bow. 'When the light shines brightly upon the shallow water, there cannot be very much to fear.' Lily gives another bow.

The couple look at each other and grin, then the woman looks back to the guidebook, as though expecting to find some explanation for Lily on the next page.

Lily skips on.

'Excuse me?' says the woman.

Lily turns around.

'Could you say that again?'

For a moment Lily has forgotten what she said. It's all nonsense, the titbits she throws to tourists; stuff she makes up on the spot.

'When the light shines brightly upon the shallow water' – she pauses but remembers just in time – 'there cannot be very much to fear.'

The woman writes this down in a leather-bound journal she has pulled from her bag. 'Is it a proverb?' she says.

Lily nods. The man reaches for his wallet and hands Lily a dollar bill, which she dutifully collects.

'Do you have another?' he says, looking at the woman, who nods in encouragement.

Lily looks at the sky as though waiting for its wisdom to descend.

'The mind sees only what the eyes are willing to comprehend.'

The man hands her another dollar while the woman makes quick notes in book. She looks up at Lily and then writes something else.

'Thank you,' says the woman, closing her book. Though Lily does not wait to see how long it takes them to cross the waterfall, she can hear them muttering to one another until their voices fade through the distance.

The nonsense proverbs began when Granny Bud was going through a particularly difficult time with the mountain spirits. She was trying so hard to communicate with them that she had very little energy for making the teas and tonics that formed the basis of her income.

'They aren't happy, Lily,' she said one night as Lily was chopping vegetables for soup.

'When have they ever been happy?' said Lily. 'Not in my lifetime.'

It wasn't that Lily didn't believe in the spirits; simply that they seemed to have no place in her life. She accepted and knew them as part of Granny Bud, whom she loved very much, but to her they seemed remote: a foreign language.

'You don't take me seriously,' said Granny Bud. 'You're too much like them.'

She meant the tourists.

Lily went over to Granny Bud where she sat on a small, wooden stool at the kitchen door, looking out over the back garden and across the mountain. She draped her arms over Granny Bud's shoulders and round her neck.

'That's not true,' said Lily, then: 'I'm sorry.'

Granny Bud untangled Lily's arms and pulled her outside so they were facing one another, Granny on the stool and Lily crouching on the wet grass.

Granny Bud gave Lily a long, hard look.

'I only meant . . .' Lily began. 'I only meant that I don't remember a time when the spirits were content.'

At this, Granny Bud became sad. 'No, no, no,' she said. 'It's them,' she said. 'There are too many of them.'

Lily went back into the kitchen, pulled a bucket full of green beans from the sink and began slicing off the ends with her thumbnails. Granny Bud was watching her and Lily nodded, trying to say that she understood, though she did not. What she knew was that there were fewer beans than usual, less food in the cupboards, no eggs on the counter, and that the money Granny Bud had been making had all but stopped.

The next day, when she was out collecting bottles, she noticed that one of the men selling knick-knacks was handing out old Chinese proverbs on thin ribbons of paper, free with every purchase. As well as the discarded bottles, Lily collected these scraps, thrown away after reading. She recognised most of the proverbs – many of them Confucian – but their translations into English made them strange. Often, she thought, they did not convey anything much at all. So she started to craft her own.

167

Whenever a tourist addressed her, she would reply with a nonsense proverb.

Those who are rich of experience are fortunate in dreams.

The tree that sways the furthest in the wind will send the blossom across the sea.

The most important materials of the earth cannot be mined.

Sometimes, to seem more authentic, she would take a real Chinese proverb and muddle the verbs.

Forget and I will tell you. Remember and I will show you. Understand and I will involve you.

She performed this kind of proverb with great seriousness as she knew this would add to the comic effect. And sometimes she just changed the words altogether.

When the wind of change blew, some made walls while others were windmills.

Quickly it began to amuse her, and, what's more, the tourists loved it. They found her charming, this pretty little wise-child from the mountains. Better still, they gave her money. She fed them nonsense and they swapped it for cash, mostly dollars, that she could change with Mister Gu, who ran the ticket stall at the entrance of Blind Water Pass, or spend at the small shop where the tourists bought supplies for the hike and the locals bought peanut milk, hard-boiled eggs and noodles in soup.

Variety was the key, she discovered. Lily did not always feel like playing dumb. Sometimes she wanted to impress. She took her English assignments more seriously at school and memorised long passages of Shakespeare with a perfect American accent. If she had tired of nonsense proverbs for the day, she pulled out a sonnet or a soliloquy and performed it in full, giving a small bow at the end. However, when the tourists tried to speak with her once the performance was done, she would still pretend not to understand. Lily made them believe it was a party trick, that she couldn't speak English at all but only memorise the sounds.

Halfway down Blind Water Pass, Lily has already collected twenty-eight bottles and received tips from five tourists. She has almost reached the man with the knick-knacks and the proverbs, when a clap of thunder arrives so suddenly that Lily stops in her tracks. She looks up at the sky, which is clear and bright, and the noise comes again. It is not coming from above, she thinks, but from below: a deep vibration that sends a tremor through the earth. Lily has experienced earthquakes before but not like this. She looks around. There is no one.

She rushes down to the place where the man with the proverbs stands. He is talking frantically with another bottle collector and a woman selling cartons of juice.

'What is it?' she says, breaking their circle. 'Do you know what it is?'

'The funicular,' says the proverb man. 'They're levelling the ground at the top of the pass.'

'It's not an earthquake?' Lily asks.

'No,' says the proverb man.

'Not yet,' says the woman, moving back towards her selling spot on the other side of the pathway.

Three girls, a little older than Lily, are making their way towards them. Two are giggling about trying not to walk on any cracks. The third one walks slightly behind them, on tiptoes, as though she hardly dares to touch the ground.

Before the girls reach her, Lily turns towards home and Granny Bud.

It feels strange to be moving in this direction so early in the day. Lily is conscious of the sun being too high in the sky. She feels guilty that she does not have more to carry: her basket is less than half full. But Granny Bud might not know, as Lily had not known, that today was the day they began preparations for the funicular. She might think it was an earthquake, as Lily had, fearing there would be worse to come.

Ing greets Lily at the gate, putting her nose against her hipbone, and Lily answers with some seeds from her pocket. Ing slopes off towards the gate and Lily goes inside.

Granny Bud is lying flat on the floor in the middle of the living room. Lily kneels at her side.

'They've gone,' says Granny Bud.

'Who's gone?' says Lily.

'The spirits. The spirits have gone.'

'How?' says Lily.

'I don't know,' says Granny Bud. 'But they've gone.'

Lily helps Granny Bud to a seated position. 'Are you frightened?' she says.

'No,' says Granny Bud.

'You know it's just the dam,' says Lily. 'The tremor, the noise.'

'It's not just the dam. The dam is not just the dam. You must know that, at least.'

'Are you cross? Please don't be cross.'

'No,' says Granny Bud.

'Then what?'

'I just feel nothing. Nothing at all.'

Lily helps Granny Bud over to a chair by the window. She tucks a shawl round Granny Bud's shoulders and tells her to wait.

In the kitchen, she heats some stock with the bones still in it and brings it in a bowl to Granny Bud.

'Here,' says Lily.

She takes the bowl from Lily's hand but continues to look straight out in front of her, saying nothing while the soup goes cold.

Lily busies herself with household chores. She makes another batch of soup with the last of the vegetables. She cleans the bath and beats the dust out of the rugs in the hallway.

Just as she is filling the bucket to mop the kitchen floor, Granny Bud opens the door.

'Did you collect many bottles today?' she says.

Lily hands her the twelve dollars she made in tips, which Granny Bud places in a small wooden box on the countertop.

'You're a good girl, Lily,' she says. 'I'm going for a walk.'

'Where?' says Lily. 'I'll come with you.'

'I'm going to look for the spirits, wherever they might have gone.'

'It's almost dark.'

'I'll take a torch.'

'Let me come with you,' says Lily.

'No,' says Granny Bud. Her voice is firm.

She crosses the kitchen and opens the back door onto the garden. Lily follows her out.

'Stay here,' says Granny Bud. 'They won't come if you're there.'

Lily watches from the threshold. Granny Bud moves slowly across the garden. A soft light comes through the clouds, hinting at the moon. The outline of her head and neck begins to fur against the dim glow.

Sand

They abandoned the truck at the edge of the city and divided themselves between two jeeps. Seven men in the back of each, shoulders knocking, thighs pressed against thighs. The road soon lost its surface to potholes, boulders and the branches of fallen trees. The track they followed was dry and pale. It passed through villages and travellers' settlements, quilts of dust billowing upwards in their wake.

On the second day, the desert came into view. It was bleak: a thousand shades of ash. There was no space here for politics. Land stretched away, bare and open and lawless.

Sand

Days bled into one another. Had he been asked, he could not have said if it was Tuesday or Friday or Sunday, if it was August or September. The other men occasionally made mention of the date with regard to a birthday they had missed or the number of days since they had left, but he allowed this information to pass unacknowledged, forgetting it as soon as it reached his ears.

They drove with the windows down, dry air in their faces, sand running into sand in an endless incantation. Pitched against such a backdrop, he felt he was no more than an outline.

When night fell, it became cold. They wrapped themselves in coats and blankets and tied their scarves more tightly round their ears. Some days, they would stop at dusk and make a fire over which they could cook, where they would sit warming themselves, before they slipped back to the car, one by one, to sleep. At other times, they journeyed onwards in the dark, snacking on flatbread and rice brought from home, not knowing how much to eat and how much to save.

The driver checked the water every evening, counting the flasks and doing sums on his fingers. He poured a little petrol into each of the containers so that the chemicals burned their throats as they swallowed but the water remained safe. Bitterness lingered in their stomachs as a dull ache. One or two of them had vomited when they drank too much. They learned. No one took more than their share.

One afternoon, in the full heat of the day, they saw another jeep a short distance from the track. Their driver pulled off the road and made towards it. They came to a stop.

'Fuel,' said the driver, getting out of the car. They followed close behind. The sand burnt their feet through the soles of their shoes, shifting beneath them and eluding their grip.

The windows of the abandoned jeep were open and it was thick with dust both inside and out. The keys had been left in the ignition. The driver opened the door, took it out of gear and tried to turn the engine. It whirred but did not start so the driver got out, flicked the latch on the bonnet and peered inside. A couple of others went to help him. The rest stood with their eyes closed against the sun.

He looked out over the dunes. There were dark shapes in the sand a couple of hundred yards from where they stood. He walked closer, picked out the contours of limbs, the lines of a torso, a protruding hand or foot. He counted. Seven bodies – all men – and perhaps more beneath the surface. Six faces were veiled beneath headscarves. One was unmasked. A thin face, an aquiline nose, eyes wide open with whites yellowed. He called to the others. They uncovered the remaining six faces, regarding each one with care, fearing to see someone they once knew.

The driver gave instructions: take scarves and coats, check pockets for money. The spoils were gathered in a pile. There was a penknife, a few coins, a fistful of notes, crumpled letters. Photographs of wives and children.

'Should we bury them?' someone said.

'Don't waste your strength,' the driver replied.

That night, the wind was low. They slept on blankets spread across the sand. The vast and empty desert brought the moon and stars a little closer to earth. He poured his gaze into the darkness and was reminded of other skies from other times.

He dreamt of home.

He was standing in the doorway watching her sleep. Her body was covered by a single yellow sheet which rose and fell with her breath. The rest of the room was still. No traffic, no breeze, no voices in the yard. He touched her cheek, her skin soft against his hand, but in the moment of his relief she disintegrated like ash in his palm.

At the end of the next day, they reached a settlement. It was close to nightfall when the pale stone houses came into view. The driver said they could rest. It was safe. The streets were narrow, empty and silent.

From a passageway between two buildings, a tall man ran out in front of their car. The driver braked hard and they were flung forwards. They came to a halt at the man's feet. Then he passed them, running again, his arms swinging wildly at his sides. They watched him through the rear windscreen. Every few seconds he turned his head to look over his shoulder. There were shouts, footsteps. Three more men emerged from the passage, in faded army uniforms, guns slung over their shoulders. Two of them went after the first man. One stayed behind, yelling something at their car in a language they did not understand. The uniformed man looked hard at the jeep and made to approach it, but the driver did not wait for him to reach them. They sped forwards, tyres screaming.

They took a sharp right turn into a lane that was only just wide enough for them to pass. His head hit the window, hard, and for a moment everything was dark. When his sight returned, he saw that they had looped back onto the road on which they had come.

The others were shouting, demanding to know what was going on. They received no response. The air in the car was still hot from the day and he could not speak. He held himself upright and remained silent. A few yards from the edge of the settlement they were surrounded. Two trucks pulled in front of them, blocking their way, then two more trapped them in from behind. More men in uniform appeared, giving orders in the same unfamiliar language. This time the message was clear. Get out of the car. Keep your hands where we can see them. You're coming with us.

They were handcuffed, all except the driver, and divided between the four trucks. A few of them shouted and struggled but he was silent, head bowed, careful to avoid catching anyone's eye. During the journey that followed, every sound, every jolt of the truck made him start. He was surprised to find that the prospect of death frightened him after all.

They arrived at a prison where they were separated and placed in crowded cells. The smell was unbearable. People have died in here, he thought.

There were in excess of twenty prisoners in a cell of ten square feet; men, women and children, crouching on the earth, or standing with their backs against the walls. Heavy iron bars lay across the gate, which the guard closed behind him.

By this time it was well after dark, but no one in the cell seemed to want to sleep. Mothers sat cradling children too tired to cry. Men stood. They were deathly thin, their skin grey.

Morning came. More guards went by. At around noon, they were taken from their cells and marched into an open yard. On all sides, uniformed men stood ready with guns. The prisoners were led to a counter where they each received a handful of cold rice before being escorted back and locked in.

An hour or so later, the driver came to see him.

'It's going to be OK. You can leave if you pay,' the driver said. 'That's all they want.'

'How much?' he said.

'How much do you have?' said the driver.

He had enough. So did four of the others. They left with the driver on the morning of the third day. Three of their party remained. He had been right, he thought, not to know them.

Sand

The air in the jeep was stifling. He tensed at the slam of the doors. No one spoke. He was ashamed in ways he could not explain. Layers had been stripped away. The outside world seemed more luminous than before, the arched lines of the desert razor sharp. The sky was a deep, planetary blue; the sun a bright white disk. It emanated something more than light; a force unknowable and relentless. There were no allies. Even the land had turned against them.

He felt only exhaustion. No fear or hope remained. He would allow the days to pass one after the other. He would make no demands, ask no questions and he did not listen to the information the driver bestowed. As they drove, his eyes clung to rocks and high dunes, anything to break the horizon.

He didn't know how many days went by, each the same as the last, until, late one night, the edge of a city emerged. Tall buildings with lit windows towered before them in the dark. Smoke rose up from factories and into the sky. There were people on the streets wearing suits and smart dresses. He felt invisible, ghostlike.

The driver took them through the suburbs, skirting

the city's checkpoints. They passed villages, farm-
land, industrial sites. They did not stop for the night.
In the morning, as the earth tipped into light, the
sea appeared on the horizon. He felt he could reach
out and touch it, feel it flowing over his fingers.
They arrived at the shore. He took off his shoes
and bathed his feet in the surf. It was less than an
hour before the boat would leave. He waited at a
distance from the others. A man in a black shirt
and trousers came to take his fare. He pulled crumpled notes from his pockets and sand fell from the
creases, through his fingers, to the earth.

The boat was no more than a dinghy, turquoise blue,
shallow and weak. They were crammed in well over
capacity. If the sea were rough, half their cargo could
be lost. He was jostled onto a bench.

They were lucky. It was calm, peaceful even. His
tiredness endured, his head thrummed and his limbs
were weak. He let his body sway and sink in time
with the movement of the waves. It had been a long
time since he had been at her side. She came to him
now and he whispered her name under his breath,
hearing nothing over the engine and the rush of the
sea. He put his fingers in his ears and tried again.

Everything is Aftermath

The day before the dragon boat festival, Wen is waiting at the bus station for the eight o'clock to Deyang. Scattered among the crowds of travellers are street vendors selling *zongzi* for the holiday — pyramids of sticky rice wrapped in bamboo leaves and secured with coloured string. Wen watches their nimble fingers weaving the leaves into parcels and is lulled by the rhythm of their movements. She is not hungry but she buys a bottle of lemon tea from a woman with an icebox slung over her shoulder. Wen hands the woman a fistful of jiao notes and takes the dewy bottle. She twists the yellow lid back and forth in her fingers. Passengers push past her, in search of other buses to other places. Watching them swarm about her makes her dizzy, so she looks up at the sky. Wen holds her chin high and breathes in, trying to catch a wave of fresher air on the breeze.

A book of poems by Hai Zi sits at the top of her rucksack. She longs to take it out, if only to look at the frames of white space protecting the words on each page. But with the pressing crowds, she fears that the book would soon be knocked from her hands. She pictures this: the book falling, being trampled and kicked along the ground, until someone picks it up. She wonders if this person would keep it and read it, or rip the pages from the spine to make swans and paper aeroplanes, or cast it back into the dirt.

When the bus pulls up to the bay it is newer than Wen expects. The seats have high upholstered backs in place of the metal barred benches she is used to. The ticket lady disembarks and passengers gather about her. The driver squeezes through the crowd and leans against the front of the bus, a cigarette clamped between his teeth. Wen watches the smoke rise until it dissolves into the white sky. Chongqing, in the wet heat of late May, is enveloped in a thick and breathless smog. She hopes the bus will make a stop some place where she can glimpse a patch of sky. Weeks of cloud weigh heavy and she craves the sun; not its warmth, but the clarity of its light.

She hands her ticket to the lady then climbs aboard and finds she has a window seat near the back. A boy – perhaps a few years older than her – is blocking the aisle. His ears are stoppered with blue rubber headphones that produce a tinny, rattling sound. It reminds her of the metal gates at her school, the way they clatter in the breeze.

She taps him on the arm and points to the seat she's trying to reach.

'I can hear that,' she says.

'What?' he says, taking a few steps back, tugging at the blue plastic cords with both hands in order to unplug his ears.

'I can hear your music. It's loud.'

To her surprise, he apologises and, without asking, lifts the bag from her shoulders and places it in the luggage rack. Wen shuffles into her seat and the boy takes the empty one at her side as the bus pulls out of the forecourt.

He flicks tracks on his iPod as they make their way through the suburbs, ancient villages dissolving into urban sprawl. Office blocks stand next to small-town farms: bankers look out over pigsties and computer manufacturers watch as grain from the fields is

collected in rush-woven baskets. As they move deeper
into the country, Wen is glad to find the roar of the
city fading. She notices that the sound coming from
the boy's headphones is now the faint swell of violins
over piano, but the volume is low and she can't find
the tune. His eyes are closed and Wen wonders at his
ability to sleep in spite of the frequent bends in the
road and the uneven terrain. When she looks back
to the window, the sky is grey and the landscape
veiled with steady summer rain.

Wen had called her mother from the pay phone at
school to say she would not be coming home for the
festival; that she would, instead, be making the six-
hour trip west to spend the three days of holiday
with Aunt Lin. Her mother took the news coolly:
  'How old are you now? Fifteen?'
  'Fifteen.' Wen knew what was coming.
  'At that age your grandmother was married and
running the factory restaurant, while your grandfather
drank himself to death. I'd say you're old enough to
do what you want and, no doubt, so would she.' Wen's
mother liked to use the legend she had built around
Wen's grandmother – her work ethic, her steeliness,
her strength – to underpin her own opinions. More

often than not, when Wen spoke to her mother, she felt she was talking to both of them.

Aunt Lin remembered Wen's grandmother in a different light. Her anecdotes were of long hours in the restaurant, relentless lists of chores and the burn of a slap on the backs of their thighs when things went wrong. Wen, having never met her grandmother, preferred to picture her as two separate beings. One a heroic pillar of strength; the other a ragged, fearsome creature.

For many years, Wen's mother and Aunt Lin had been close. After they were married, they lived on the same street in Guo village for almost ten years. They gave birth to daughters, Wen and Mei Li, in the same cold December. Wen's parents ran the factory restaurant, Mr Lin worked in the factory itself and Aunt Lin stayed at home to take care of Wen and Mei Li. When Wen's mother got back from the late evening shift, she liked to sit with Aunt Lin, brewing and rebrewing the same dark tea leaves. Wen would creep out of bed and watch them as they whispered over the pot, holding the patterned china teacups close to their lips.

Things began to change when Mr Lin got a promotion and moved Aunt Lin and Mei Li across the province to Deyang. Without Aunt Lin, Wen had to go to the factory restaurant before and after school. She sat and watched the workers as they ate. When it was busy, she carried them bowls of steaming noodle soup, swept the floors, wiped the tables and kept quiet. Her mother never asked if she missed Mei Li and Wen sensed she was not to ask too many questions about Mei Li and Aunt Lin.

From time to time they came to visit, Aunt Lin driving Mei Li and herself in the car that Mr Lin had bought her. Aunt Lin would say little during these visits but Mei Li would be the same as always: flippant and gregarious, playing with her hair, making mish-mash outfits in clashing colours. She loved to sing and cook and eat. She was a chatterbox, a scatterbrain and a glutton. Wherever she was, the room moved inevitably in her orbit.

She and Wen would go walking by the river and leave behind them the sound of Wen's mother saying how fortunate Mei Li was. Now that Mr Lin had got his promotion, Mei Li would have such bright opportunities before her. She could spend her summers abroad, learn ballet or take piano lessons after school.

'Just what would her grandmother have made of all this,' Wen's mother would say.

At the first of their rest stops, the boy beside her alights. Wen remains on board and takes out her book, reading a few lines while she can do so without making herself travel-sick. The boy returns to his seat with a bag of fresh green dates.

'Want one?' he says.

'No, thanks.'

He puts a date into his mouth, chews it, swallows. 'I'm Tian,' he says.

Wen nods and Tian smiles. When it seems he is not going to ask her name in return, she says: 'I'm Wen,' and closes the book of poems between her palms.

At each of the stops after that, Tian buys a different snack from a station shop or roadside stall. He comes back with dried pork, steamed buns, red bean cake and candied gourds, offering each of his purchases to her. When she refuses, he puts the unopened packages into a pocket at the top of his rucksack. Wen wonders if he will eat them later, throw them away or dish them out for someone else. She spends their breaks snatching lines from her book while the rain continues to pour.

It is two years since Mei Li's funeral. Wen's mother and Aunt Lin had not seen each other for some time when the earthquake struck. Mei Li was crushed beneath the ceiling of the music room at her school. When they found her body it was bloodied and bruised, the left side of her face collapsed to a pulp. Aunt Lin said it was best Wen hadn't seen.

At the funeral, Wen embraced Aunt Lin, and felt a stiff jerk in her shoulders as Aunt Lin clasped her tightly in her arms. Other mourners went past offering words of condolence but Wen's mother offered no such comfort. Instead, she talked about the restaurant's shrinking profit margins and the pain in the small of her back. Wen was embarrassed, though she understood. Her mother worked hard and was unwilling to allow Aunt Lin a greater claim on suffering as well as wealth.

The last time Wen saw Mei Li, they were walking down by the river in Guo Village. They counted the fishing boats planted in the mud rifts. It was January, then, just before the New Year, and they blew their breath into the cold. In the excitement leading up to Spring Festival they talked about what they would do with the money they received in their red envelopes. Wen would buy a notebook with a padlock and a bottle of calligraphy ink. Mei Li wanted to get her nails painted like sunsets and buy a box of

Hershey chocolates from the exotic food shop in Chengdu.

Wen had just pointed to the twelfth mud-covered boat when Aunt Lin drove up beside them. She said it was time for her to take Mei Li home. When Mei Li didn't move, Aunt Lin got out. Mei Li hurried into the car. The moment the door was shut, Mei Li opened the window and poked her head out. Wen hugged her through the gap and found that her eyes met Aunt Lin's. They stayed there looking at one another until Mei Li unhooked her arms from around Wen's neck and turned to face Aunt Lin, her permission for them to leave.

Aunt Lin has not been back to Guo Village since Mei Li's death, but she sometimes visits Wen in Chongqing. She stays at a hotel on the same road as Wen's school. When she takes Wen out for dinner, it is clear that she has poured her heart into the idea of procuring a new child. Her only hope lies with *in vitro* fertilisation. On her last visit, Aunt Lin explained to Wen that she was now a patient at the best fertility clinic in the whole of the provincial capital. She was more hopeful than ever, she said. She had seen several women walk into the waiting room in triumph, clutching newborns to their breasts; bringing their tiny, screaming trophies to meet the doctor who had conjured them into being.

When the bus pulls into Deyang at around three o'clock in the afternoon, Tian asks if Wen would like to share his taxi. She tells him that her aunt is picking her up. Tian shrugs and gets into the car. She sees him turn and look back at her through the rear windscreen as the cab pulls out into the road. Wen waits on the pavement. She has crossed two hundred miles of countryside without once glimpsing the unclouded light of the sun.

It is Mr Lin who collects her. He is dressed in brown: carefully pressed brown trousers, bobbles appearing on his brown cotton shirt.

'Hello, little niece,' he says, placing a hand on her shoulder. She gets in the car. 'I'm afraid your Aunt Lin isn't feeling very well.'

When they arrive at the apartment, Wen is greeted by the sound of vomiting.

'There was a last-minute cancellation at the clinic,' Mr Lin explains. 'We were there all morning.'

'Can she be pregnant already?' Wen whispers and Mr Lin laughs without smiling.

'It's the injections. They make her sick.'

Wen crosses the apartment to the bedroom. Aunt Lin is perched on the far side of the bed in a loose robe of lilac satin. She looks over her shoulder and tries to smile at Wen before she retches again. Wen kneels on the bed behind her and strokes her back. She runs her hands between Aunt Lin's shoulder blades, smoothing the folds of the satin robe. Wen lets her fingers rest at the nape of her neck as Aunt Lin wretches over the plastic bowl at her feet.

When the vomiting stops, it is late in the evening and Mr Lin has gone out. With her aunt in bed, Wen is alone. She wanders into Mei Li's room. On the walls there are patches of different-coloured paint. Mei Li's school books remain in a neat pile on the desk and Mei Li's slippers rest by the side of the bed. Wen leafs through the notebook at the top of the pile and sees a list of English verbs. Each one has been copied out several times.

I am, you am, he is, we are, they are.
I am, you are, he are, we are, they are.
I am, you are, he is, we are, they are.

In her Senior Two English class, Wen is reading Hemingway. She returns Mei Li's book to the pile and pulls out the spare mattress from behind the wardrobe. She takes the mattress into the study and makes a bed for herself there, not wanting to disturb Mei Li's spirit.

On the morning of Double Fifth, Aunt Lin rises early and, long before Wen lifts herself from the mattress, there is the sound of singing from the kitchen. Wen gets up to join her aunt and is ushered to the table with a cup of hot soya milk. Aunt Lin puts a basket of sweet, deep-fried dough sticks and a dragon fruit on the table. They sit together flaking off pieces of sugared pastry with their fingers, dipping them into the milk. Neither one of them manages to consume very much of the dough but both remember Mei Li's taste for it. Eventually they give up and halve the dragon fruit, prising out the speckled flesh with teaspoons.

'What's it like at the clinic?' says Wen.

'It's lovely,' says Aunt Lin, smiling. 'I feel very well taken care of.'

'Is it busy?' says Wen. 'Do a lot of women go?'

Aunt Lin nods. 'A lot of people lost children.'

'So everyone's there because of the earthquake?'

'I asked the doctor that,' says Aunt Lin. 'I asked him if everyone was there, like me, in the aftermath of the earthquake.'

'What did he say?'

'He said: "Mrs Lin, there will always be disasters. Earthquakes, miscarriages, whatever." Then he said something about things happening and people reacting in the best way they could think of. He said: "Everything we do happens in the aftermath of something else, wouldn't you say? Our whole lives are the aftermath of something." I couldn't think of anything to say after that, so he did the injections and I came home.'

Aunt Lin is standing over the stove, removing bamboo-wrapped rice parcels from a pan of simmering water. She places them in a large red box with chopsticks, then she seals the box with a metal lid.

Wen and Aunt Lin walk into the city centre. By the time they have snaked their way through the crowds that fill the streets and reached the banks of the Jinghu River, the dragon boat race is already over. The long boats are tethered to the bank, bobbing up and down in the current. Brightly clad rowers are receiving their medals on a podium at the foot of the bridge.

When they find a place along the strand, Aunt Lin produces the box of dumplings from her bag. Slowly, without speaking, they take the bamboo parcels and let them fall, one by one, into the river. All along its banks, as far as Wen can see, children are making similar offerings to the water.

A singer, an *erhu* player and a *yangqin* pianist mount the podium to perform 'Mo Li Hua'. As the familiar melody pours forth, a little girl standing next to Wen jumps with excitement. The girl, about three years old, has high, tufty pigtails and is dressed in a pair of bright-red dungarees. She has a stack of plastic bangles up her arm and about her neck are multiple strings of beads, long enough to reach her knees. When the chorus comes, she sways from side to side and the beads swing wildly. While the last note is ringing clear in the air, the girl's mother bundles her child into her arms and makes to leave. The girl screams and struggles in protest, sending one of her many bangles tumbling to the ground. Aunt Lin stoops to retrieve the trinket then looks back at the girl, who is now walking, led by her mother's hand, into the thick of the crowd. Aunt Lin tucks the bangle into her handbag. Wen pretends not to have seen.

At four o'clock, the crowds thin as the festivities come to a close. Wen and Aunt Lin walk to the earthquake memorial. Aunt Lin buys a bunch of white lilies from a florist's stall at the gate. The approach to the

memorial is through an orchard along a narrow gravel
path, lined with wreaths and bouquets.

'Were there this many flowers before?' Wen asks.

'It's because of the anniversary. A week ago it was
two years ago,' says Aunt Lin, 'if you see what I mean.'

The memorial stone is an obelisk set on a wide
circular plinth where more flowers are laid. Some
are fresh but most are fake and moulding petals
make a dark carpet for the bright silk blooms. Aunt
Lin places her bouquet of lilies over someone else's
dying freesias. Wen looks up at the stone and reads
the words of condolence. Her gaze wanders from the
inscription and she sees Tian standing on the far
side of the plinth. He takes a step towards her and
opens his mouth as if to speak, but then looks across
at Aunt Lin. Wen turns to see that her aunt has
buried her face in her hands. She doesn't appear to
be crying so much as blocking the world from view.
Wen places a hand on Aunt Lin's shoulder then looks
back at Tian. He raises a hand in greeting. Wen
mirrors the gesture and they stand for several
seconds, taking in one another's gaze. Then Tian
turns to leave and, as he walks into the orchard,
Wen wraps her arms round her aunt.

When they get back to the apartment, Mr Lin is
asleep. They can hear him snoring through the closed

bedroom door. There is a dirty plate and a couple of empty Tsingtao bottles by the side of the kitchen sink.

'He has eaten already,' says Aunt Lin in a tired voice. She goes to take a nap in Mei Li's room. Wen steams spinach with Sichuan peppercorns and sesame then lays soft triangles of tofu in a pan of oil with ginger and garlic. At the back of the store cupboard, between a sack of rice and a box of cabbages, is a lumpy muslin bag tied up with string. Wen pulls it into the light. Waiting for the tofu to cook, she sits cross-legged on the kitchen floor and rests the bag on her ankles. She teases the knot free and puts a hand in to rummage through the contents. She pulls out the items one by one. A plastic doll missing an eye. A yo-yo without its string. A cracked mobile-phone cover with stick-on plastic jewels. A half-finished cross-stitch pattern of pink and purple flowers, with loose threads pinned to the fabric. A handful of bright plastic beads for weaving into the ends of hair braids. Wen places the items in a line in front of her.

She looks for a long time at the collection. Had these things once belonged to Mei Li? She remembered Mei Li wearing beads in her hair, but was sure they had been gold. Wen didn't think that Mei Li had ever owned a mobile phone, though it was likely that if she had it would have had that sort of cover:

something shiny with lots of bright colours. Then Wen remembers the girl from the riverside and the bangle in Aunt Lin's handbag. Wen returns the objects to the bag with care and replaces the string tie at the top. She puts the bag back where she found it, wedged between the rice and the cabbages.

After dinner, Wen makes tea and Aunt Lin decides to sleep in Mei Li's room. Wen sits with her awhile, going through Mei Li's books, reading the poems she copied from textbooks to learn by heart. She examines the hotchpotch paint strips on the wall, but can't pick a favourite colour. When she gets tired, Wen picks up a couple of Mei Li's English books and takes them into the study. Lying on the mattress, she flicks through the pages until she falls asleep.

In the morning, Wen and Aunt Lin breakfast on congee with chilli and pickles. Aunt Lin busies herself preparing a selection of small tupperware boxes filled with food for Wen to take on the journey. In order to be back inside the school gates before dark, Wen must catch the twelve o'clock bus.

'When will you know,' asks Wen. She is kneeling by the mattress in the study, rolling up clothes and putting them back in her rucksack.

'In a week or two perhaps, but even then, it's not . . .' she breaks off, 'It's not *secure*.'

Wen nods, hesitates. 'And what if it's a boy?' she almost whispers.

'What do you mean?'

Wen raises her voice a little: 'I mean what will you do if it's a boy?'

'I don't even know if I'm pregnant, yet,' says Aunt Lin.

'But would you want a boy?'

'I guess not.'

'Well then,' says Wen. There is a pause.

'I'd teach him to cook.'

'To cook?'

'Mei Li would like that.'

Wen packs the last of her clothes into the bag and zips it shut. She slips Mei Li's English books into a pocket at the front. Aunt Lin comes in holding three Tupperware boxes. She hands them to Wen one by one.

'Dragon fruit, rice balls, and pumpkin cakes,' she says. Wen opens her rucksack again and packs them in on top of her clothes.

Sitting in the car at the bus station, Aunt Lin takes Wen's hand in hers and smoothes a couple of one-hundred yuan notes into Wen's palm.

'Thank you,' says Wen. 'You don't have to.'

'I know.'

Wen nods. 'Let me know, if—'

'Of course.'

'And I'll come back soon.'

Wen looks around. They are twenty minutes early but the twelve o'clock bus to Chonqging is already sitting in bay five. Wen kisses Aunt Lin on the cheek and gets out of the car. The station is quiet. On one of the benches near bay five she sees Tian. He is sitting with his eyes closed and his rucksack at his feet. She turns to watch Aunt Lin's car pull out of the station and into the street, then looks back to the bench.

Tian opens his eyes. She walks over to his bench.

'Is this your bus? The twelve o'clock?' Wen asks.

'I guess so,' says Tian. 'I just need to buy my ticket.'

Wen climbs aboard. She takes off her rucksack and places it in the luggage rack above. A minute later, Tian takes the seat beside her.

After almost an hour, the bus makes a stop. Tian disembarks and Wen retrieves Mei Li's English book and one of the Tupperware boxes from her bag. She opens the book to find a table of past-tense verb conjugations.

I am, I was, I had been.
You are, you were, you had been.
He is, he were, he had been.
We is, we were, we had been.
They is, they were, they had been.

Wen takes a pencil from her pocket and begins correcting the errors. When Tian returns to his seat, Wen opens the Tupperware box. Inside there are thick slices of dragon fruit.

'Want one?' she says, and he takes a large chunk between his finger and thumb. The bus pulls back onto the road.

They move out into the countryside, dirt roads and small villages in the distance. With Mei Li's book still open on her lap, Wen and Tian eat slice after slice of the speckled white fruit. The juice runs down Wen's hand and over her wrist, blurring the ink as it hits the pages.

Acknowledgements

Thank you Henry, Philip, Karolina, Mark, Kirsten, Rebecca, Rachel, Anna J, Sara and Mike, for making things possible. Thank you, especially, Beryl and Michael (Ma and Pa): to you I owe the entirety of my literary education. Your love and kindness have given me the generosity of imagination.

Thank you to the following publications where stories from this collection first appeared:

'Number Three' has previously been published in Lighthouse Journal Issue 2, in *The Best of British Short Stories 2014* (Salt) and in *Six Shorts 2014: The Sunday Times EFG Short Story Award*.

'Sand' was published in *The Bath Short Story Award Anthology 2015*.

Acknowledgements

'Old Ghost' was published in the first issue of *The Lonely Crowd* in April 2015.

'Everything is Aftermath' was featured in *The Warwick Review* in March 2014.

An earlier version of 'Still' was published as 'Dark Room' online in the Wales Arts Review: http://www.walesartsreview.org/dark-room/.

'The Professor' was shortlisted for the 2014 Words and Women Short Story Prize and published in *Words and Women: Two* (Unthank Books).

An earlier version of 'Rock Sparrow' was published as 'Flight' in the e-book anthology *Good Reads: Bath Short Story Award 2013*.